"I want to kiss you."

"That's a bad idea," Tasha said.

"Why?" Matt asked.

"The signature on my paycheck. Besides, I'm not that kind of girl."

"The kind that kisses men?"

"The kind that randomly kisses men, while I'm working, in an engine room, covered in grease."

"So, are there any circumstances under which you'd agree to kiss me? Maybe if we left the engine room? Perhaps if you washed off the grease?"

"Nice try."

"I thought so."

"You're just not used to hearing the word *no*."

"You're right. It makes you even more attractive to me. Now I'm hoping against hope that you'll admit you're attracted to me."

A flush came up on her cheeks. "We both know you struck out."

"Maybe. But this is only the first inning. In fact, let's call it batting practice."

* * *

Twelve Nights of Temptation is part of the Whiskey Bay Brides series: Three friends find love on the shores of Whiskey Bay.

Dear Reader,

Welcome to the second book in the Whiskey Bay Brides series! The Pacific Northwest is one of the most beautiful places on earth. Where else can you go from skiing a snowy alpine run to swimming on a warm beach in only a few hours? The rugged beauty of Whiskey Bay is the perfect setting for romance.

In *Twelve Nights of Temptation*, marina owner Matt Emerson is the target of sabotage, which endangers both his fleet of luxury yachts and his hardworking staff. When he joins forces with his mechanic, Tasha Lowell, to catch the culprit, he finds himself seeing past her unadorned exterior to find a gorgeous woman beneath. But Tasha refuses to compromise her hard-won respect by dating the boss.

Then the stakes grow higher when Tasha becomes the target, and she and Matt are thrown together—at sea with no one to depend on but each other.

Barbara

BARBARA DUNLOP

TWELVE NIGHTS OF TEMPTATION

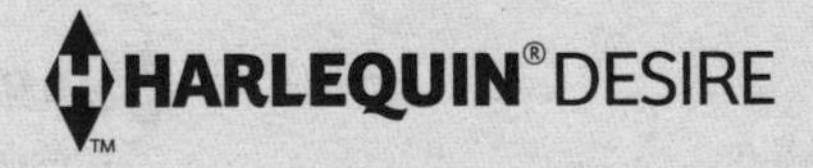

Recycling programs for this product may not exist in your area.

ISBN-13: 978-0-373-83882-0

Twelve Nights of Temptation

This edition published by arrangement with Harlequin Books S.A.

For questions and comments about the quality of this book, please contact us at CustomerService@Harlequin.com.

Printed in U.S.A.

New York Times and *USA TODAY* bestselling author **Barbara Dunlop** has written more than forty novels for Harlequin, including the acclaimed Chicago Sons series for Harlequin Desire. Her sexy, lighthearted stories regularly hit bestseller lists. Barbara is a three-time finalist for the Romance Writers of America's RITA® Award.

Books by Barbara Dunlop

Harlequin Desire

One Baby, Two Secrets

Chicago Sons

Sex, Lies and the CEO
Seduced by the CEO
A Bargain with the Boss
His Stolen Bride

Whiskey Bay Brides

From Temptation to Twins
Twelve Nights of Temptation

Visit her Author Profile page at Harlequin.com, or barbaradunlop.com, for more titles.

For Jane Porter

One

A banging on Tasha Lowell's bedroom door jarred her awake. It was midnight in the Whiskey Bay Marina staff quarters, and she'd been asleep for less than an hour.

"Tasha?" Marina owner Matt Emerson's voice was a further jolt to her system, since she'd been dreaming about him.

"What is it?" she called out, then realized he'd never hear her sleep-croaky voice. "What?" she called louder as she forced herself from beneath the covers.

It might be unseasonably warm on the Pacific Northwest coast, but it was still December, the holiday season, and the eight-unit staff quarters building had been around since the '70s.

"*Orca's Run* broke down off Tyree, Oregon."

"What happened?" she asked reflexively as she crossed the cold wooden floor on her bare feet. Even as she said the words, she knew it was a foolish question. Wealthy, urbane Matt Emerson wouldn't know an injector pump from an alternator.

She swung the door open, coming face-to-face with

the object of what she suddenly remembered had been a very R-rated dream.

"The engine quit. Captain Johansson says they're anchored in the bay."

This was very bad news. Tasha had been chief mechanic at Whiskey Bay Marina for less than two weeks, and she knew Matt had hesitated in giving her the promotion. He'd be right to hold her responsible for not noticing a problem with *Orca's Run*'s engine or not anticipating some kind of wear and tear.

"I serviced it right before they left." She knew how important this particular charter was to the company.

Orca's Run was a ninety-foot yacht, the second largest in the fleet. It had been chartered by Hans Reinstead, an influential businessman out of Munich. Matt had recently spent considerable effort and money getting a toehold in the European market, and Hans was one of his first major clients. The last thing Whiskey Bay Marina needed was for the Reinstead family to have a disappointing trip.

Tasha grabbed the red plaid button-down shirt she'd discarded on a chair and put it on over her T-shirt. Then she stepped into a pair of heavy cargo pants, zipping them over her flannel shorts.

Matt watched her progress as she popped a cap on top of her braided hair. Socks and work boots took her about thirty seconds, and she was ready.

"That's it?" he asked.

"What?" She didn't understand the question.

"You're ready to go?"

She glanced down at herself, then looked back into the dim bedroom. "I'm ready." The necessities that most women carried in a purse were in the zipped pockets of her pants.

For some reason, he gave a crooked smile. "Then let's go."

"What's funny?" she asked as she fell into step beside him.

"Nothing."

They started down the wooden walkway that led to the Whiskey Bay Marina pier.

"You're laughing," she said.

"I'm not."

"You're laughing at me." Did she look that bad rolling straight out of bed? She rubbed her eyes, lifted her cap to smooth her hair and tried to shake some more sense into her brain.

"I'm smiling. It's not the same thing."

"I've amused you." Tasha hated to be amusing. She wanted people, especially men, *especially* her employer, to take her seriously.

"You impressed me."

"By getting dressed?"

"By being efficient."

She didn't know what to say to that. It wasn't quite sexist…maybe…

She let it drop.

They went single file down the ramp with him in the lead.

"What are we taking?" she asked.

"Monty's Pride."

The answer surprised her. *Monty's Pride* was the biggest yacht in the fleet, a 115-footer, refurbished last year to an impeccably high standard. It was obvious what Matt intended to do.

"Do you think we'll need to replace *Orca's Run*?" She'd prefer to be optimistic and take the repair boat instead. *Monty's Pride* would burn an enormous amount of fuel getting to Tyree. "There's a good chance I can fix whatever's gone wrong."

"And if you can't?"

"What did the captain say happened?" She wasn't ready to admit defeat before they'd even left the marina.

"That it quit."

It was a pathetic amount of information.

"Did it stop all of a sudden?" she asked. "Did it slow? Was there any particular sound, a smell? Was there smoke?"

"I didn't ask."

"You should have asked."

Matt shot her a look of impatience, and she realized she'd stepped over the line. He was her boss after all.

"I'm just thinking that taking *Monty's Pride* is a whole lot of fuel to waste," she elaborated on her thinking. "We can save the money if I can do a quick repair."

"We're not even going to try a quick repair. I'll move the passengers and crew over to *Monty's Pride* while you fix whatever's gone wrong."

Tasha hated that her possible negligence would cost the company so much money. "Maybe if I talk to the captain on the radio."

"I don't want to mess around, Tasha." Matt punched in the combination for the pier's chain-link gate and swung it open.

"I'm not asking you to mess around. I'm suggesting we explore our options. *Monty's Pride* burns a hundred gallons an hour."

"My priority is customer service."

"This is expensive customer service."

"Yes, it is."

His tone was flat, and she couldn't tell if he was angry or not.

She wished she was back in her dream. Matt had been so nice in her dream. They'd been warm, cocooned together, and he'd been joking, stroking her hair, kissing her mouth.

Wait. No. That was bad. That wasn't what she wanted at all.

"I want Hans Reinstead to go back to Germany a happy man," Matt continued. "I want him to rave to his friends and business associates about the over-the-top service he received, even when there was a problem. Whether we fix it in five minutes or five hours is irrelevant. They had a breakdown, and we upgraded them. People love an upgrade. So much so, that they're generally willing to gloss over the reason for getting it."

Tasha had to admit it was logical. It was expensive, but it was also logical.

Matt might be willing to take the financial hit in the name of customer service, but if it turned out to be something she'd missed, it would be a black mark against her.

They approached the slip where *Monty's Pride* was moored. A crew member was on deck while another was on the wharf, ready to cast off.

"Fuel?" Matt asked the young man on deck.

"Three thousand gallons."

"That'll do," Matt said as he crossed the gangway to the stern of the main deck.

Tasha followed. *Monty's Pride*'s twin diesel engines rumbled beneath them.

"Is my toolbox on board?" she asked.

"We put it in storage."

"Thanks." While they crossed the deck, she reviewed *Orca's Run*'s engine service in her mind. Had she missed something, a belt or a hose? She thought she'd checked them all. But nobody's memory was infallible.

"It could be as simple as a belt," she said to Matt.

"That will be good news." He made his way to the bridge, and she followed close behind.

She had to give it one last shot, so as soon as they were inside, she went for the radio, dialing in the company frequency. "*Orca's Run*, this is *Monty's Pride*. Captain, are you there?"

While she did that, he slid open the side window and called out to the hand to cast off.

She keyed the mike again. "Come in, *Orca's Run*."

Matt brought up the revs and pulled away from the pier.

Matt knew he had taken a gamble by using *Monty's Pride* instead of the repair boat, but so far it looked like it had been the right call. Two hours into the trip down the coast, even Tasha had been forced to admit a quick fix wasn't likely. She'd had Captain Johansson walk her through a second-by-second rehash of the engine failure over the radio, asking him about sounds, smells and warning lights. Then she had him send a deckhand back and forth from the engine room for a visual inspection and to relay details.

He'd been impressed by her thorough, methodical approach. But in the end, she concluded that she needed to check the engine herself. There was nothing to do for the next three hours but make their way to Tyree.

It was obvious she was ready to blame herself.

But even if the breakdown turned out to be her fault, it wasn't the end of the world. And they didn't even know what had happened. It was way too early to start pointing fingers.

"You should lie down for a while," he told her.

She looked tired, and there was no point in both of them staying up all night.

"I'm fine." She lifted her chin, gazing out the windshield into the starry night.

There were clusters of lights along the shore, only a few other ships in the distance, and his GPS and charts were top-notch. It was an easy chore to pilot the boat single-handed.

"You don't have to keep me company."

"And you don't have to coddle me."

"You have absolutely nothing to prove, Tasha." He knew she took pride in her work, and he knew she was determined to do a good job after her promotion. But sleep deprivation wasn't a job requirement.

"I'm not trying to prove anything. Did you get any sleep at all? Do you want to lie down?"

"I'm fine." He knew she was perfectly capable of piloting the boat, but he'd feel guilty leaving all the work to her.

"No need for us both to stay awake," she said.

"My date ended early. I slept a little."

Since his divorce had been finalized, Matt and his friend TJ Bauer had hit the Olympia social circuit. They were pushing each other to get out and meet new people. They met a few women, most were nice, but he hadn't felt a spark with any of them, including the one he'd taken out tonight. He'd come home early, done a little Christmas shopping online for his nieces and nephews and dozed off on the sofa.

"You don't need to tell me about your dates," Tasha said.

"There's nothing to tell."

"Well, that's too bad." Her tone was lighter. It sounded like she was joking. "It might help pass the time."

"Sorry," he said lightly in return. "I wish I could be more entertaining. What about you?" he asked.

As he voiced the question, he found himself curious about Tasha's love life. Did she have a boyfriend? Did she date? She was always such a no-nonsense fixture at the marina, he didn't think of her beyond being a valued employee.

"What about me?" she asked.

"Do you ever go out?"

"Out where?"

"Out, out. On-a-date out. Dinner, dancing…"

She scoffed out a laugh.

"Is that a no?"

"That's a no."

"Why not?" Now he was really curious. She might dress in plain T-shirts and cargo pants, but underneath what struck him now as a disguise, she was a lovely woman. "Don't you like to dress up? Do you ever dress up?"

He tried to remember if he'd ever seen her in anything stylish. He couldn't, and he was pretty sure he'd remember.

She shifted on the swivel chair, angling toward him. "Why the third degree?"

"Since stories of my dates won't distract us, I thought maybe yours could." He found himself scrutinizing her face from an objective point of view.

She had startling green eyes, the vivid color of emeralds or a glacial, deep-water pond. They were framed in thick lashes. Her cheekbones were high. Her chin was the perfect angle. Her nose was narrow, almost delicate. And her lips were deep coral, the bottom slightly fuller than the top.

He wanted to kiss them.

"Nothing to tell," she said. Her voice jolted him back to reality, and he turned to the windshield, rewinding the conversation.

"You must dress up sometimes."

"I prefer to focus on work."

"Why?"

"Because it's satisfying." Her answer didn't ring true.

He owned the company, and he still found time for a social life. "I dress up. I date. I still find time to work."

She made a motion with her hand, indicating up and down his body. "Of course you date. A guy like you is definitely going to date."

He had no idea what she meant. "A guy like me?"

"Good-looking. Rich. Eligible."

"Good-looking?" He was surprised that she thought so, even more surprised that she'd said so.

She rolled her eyes. "It's not me, Matt. The world thinks you're good-looking. Don't pretend you've never noticed."

He'd never given it much thought. Looks were so much a matter of taste. He was fairly average. He'd never thought there was anything wrong with being average.

"I'm eligible now," he said.

The rich part was also debatable. He hadn't had enough money to satisfy his ex-wife. And now that they'd divorced, he had even less. He'd borrowed money to pay her out, and he was going to have to work hard over the next year or two to get back to a comfortable financial position.

"And so are you," he said to Tasha. "You're intelligent, hardworking and pretty. You should definitely be out there dating."

He couldn't help but compare her with the women he'd met lately. The truth was, they couldn't hold a candle to her. There was so much about her that was compelling. Funny that he'd never noticed before.

"Dazzle them with your intelligence and hard work."

"Can we not do this?" she asked.

"Make conversation?"

"I'm a licensed marine mechanic. And I want people to take me seriously as that."

"You can't do both?"

"Not in my experience." She slipped down from the high white leather chair.

"What are you doing?" he asked. He didn't want her to leave.

"I'm going to take your advice."

"What advice is that?"

"I'm going to lie down and rest." She glanced at her watch. "You think two hours?"

"I didn't mean to chase you away."

"You didn't."

"We don't have to talk about dating." But then he took in her pursed lips and realized he still wanted to kiss them. Where was this impulse coming from?

"I have work to do when we get there."

He realized he'd be selfish to stop her. "You're right. You should get some sleep."

As she walked away, he considered the implications of being attracted to an employee. He couldn't act on it. He shouldn't act on it.

Then he laughed at himself. It wasn't like she'd given him any encouragement. Well, other than saying he was good-looking.

She thought he was good-looking.

As he piloted his way along the dark coastline, he couldn't help but smile.

Tasha's problem wasn't dating in general. Her problem was the thought of dating Matt. He wasn't her type.

There was no way he was her type. She knew that for an absolute fact.

She'd dated guys like him before—capable, confident, secure in the knowledge that the world rolled itself out at their feet. She knew all that. Still, she couldn't seem to stop herself from dreaming about him.

They'd arrived off Tyree and boarded *Orca's Run* shortly after dawn. Tall and confident, he'd greeted the clients like he owned the place—which he did, of course.

Tasha had kept to the background, making sure her toolbox was moved discreetly on board, while Matt had charmed the family, apologizing for the delay in the trip, offering *Monty's Pride* as a replacement, explaining that the larger, faster yacht would easily make up the time they'd lost overnight.

It was obvious the client was delighted with the solution, and Tasha had turned her attention to the diesel engine. It took her over an hour to discover the water separator was the problem. In an unlikely coincidence, the water-in-fuel indicator light bulb had also broken. Otherwise, it would have alerted her to the fact that the water separator was full, starving the engine of fuel.

The two things happening together were surprising. They were more than surprising. They were downright strange.

From their anchorage in Tyree, Matt had taken the launch and run for parts in the small town. And by noon, she'd replaced the water separator. While she'd worked, she'd cataloged who'd had access to *Orca's Run*. Virtually all the staff of Whiskey Bay Marina had access. But most of them didn't know anything about engines.

There were a couple of contract mechanics who did repairs from time to time. And there were countless customers who had been on the property. She found her brain going in fantastical directions, imagining someone might have purposely damaged the engine.

But who? And why? And was she being ridiculously paranoid?

She had no idea.

While she'd worked, diesel fuel had sprayed her clothes and soaked into her hair, so she'd used the staff shower to clean up and commandeered a steward's uniform from the supply closet.

After cleaning up, her mind still pinging from possibility to possibility, she made her way up the stairs to the main cabin. There she was surprised to realize the yacht wasn't yet under way.

"Did something else go wrong?" she asked Matt, immediately worried they had another problem.

He was in the galley instead of piloting the yacht. The deckhand had stayed with *Monty's Pride*, since the bigger ship needed an extra crew member. Matt and Tasha were fully capable of returning *Orca's Run* to Whiskey Bay.

"It's all good," Matt said.

"We're not under power?" Her hair was still damp, and she tucked it behind her ears as she approached the countertop that separated the galley from the main living area.

"Are you hungry?" he asked, placing a pan on the stove.

She was starving. "Sure. But I can eat something on the way."

"Coffee?"

"Sure."

He extracted two cups from a cupboard and poured. "*Monty's Pride* is headed south. Everyone seems happy."

"You were right," she admitted as she rounded the counter. "Bringing *Monty's Pride* was a good idea. I can cook if you want to get going."

He gave a thoughtful nod. "This charter matters."

"Because it's a German client?"

"It's the first significant booking out of the fall trade show. He's a prominent businessman with loads of connections."

"I'm sorry I argued with you." She realized her stance had been about her pride, not about the good of the company.

"You should always say what you think."

"I should listen, too."

"You don't listen?"

"Sometimes I get fixated on my own ideas." She couldn't help but revisit her theory about someone tampering with the engine.

Matt gave a smile. "You have conviction. That's not a bad thing. Besides, it keeps the conversation interesting."

He handed her a cup of coffee.

She took a sip, welcoming the hit of caffeine.

He seemed to ponder her for a moment. "You definitely keep things interesting."

She didn't know how to respond.

His blue eyes were dark but soft, and he had an incredibly handsome face. His chin was square, unshaven and slightly shadowed, but that only made him look more rugged. His nose was straight, his jaw angular and his lips were full, dark pink, completely kissable.

Warm waves of energy seemed to stream from him to cradle her. It was disconcerting, and she shifted to put some more space between them. "The engine was interesting."

Mug to his lips, he lifted his brow.

"The odds of the water separator filling and the indicator light going at the same time are very low."

His brow furrowed then, and he lowered the mug. "And?"

"Recognizing that this is my first idea, and that I can sometimes get fixated on those, it seems wrong to me. I mean, it seems odd to me."

"Are you saying someone broke something on purpose?"

"No, I'm not saying that." Out loud, it sounded even less plausible than it had inside her head. "I'm saying it was a bizarre coincidence, and I must be having a run of bad luck."

"You fixed it, so that's good luck."

"Glass half-full?"

"You did a good job, Tasha."

"It wasn't that complicated."

A teasing glint came into his eyes. "You mean, you're that skilled?"

"The cause was peculiar." She could have sworn she'd just serviced the water separator. "The repair was easy."

Their gazes held, and they fell silent again. Raindrops clattered against the window, while the temperature seemed to inch up around her. Her dream came back once again, Matt cradling her, kissing her. Heat rose in her cheeks.

She forced herself back to the present, trying to keep her mind on an even keel. "It could have been excess water in the fuel, maybe a loose cap. I did check it. At least I think I checked it. I always check it." She paused. "I hope I checked it."

He set down his mug. "Don't."

She didn't understand.

He took a step forward. "Don't second-guess yourself."

"Okay." It seemed like the easiest answer, since she was losing track of the conversation.

He took another step, and then another.

Inside her head, she shouted for him to stop. But she didn't make a sound.

She didn't want him to stop. She could almost feel his arms around her.

He was right there.

Thunder suddenly cracked through the sky above them. A wave surged beneath them, and she grabbed for the counter. She missed, stumbling into his chest.

In a split second, his arms were around her, steadying her.

She fought the desire that fogged her brain. "Sorry."

"Weather's coming up," he said, his deep voice rumbling in her ear and vibrating her chest, which was pressed tight against his.

"We won't be—" Words failed her as she looked into his blue eyes, so close, so compelling.

He stilled, the sapphire of his eyes softening to summer sky.

"Tasha." Her name was barely a breath on his lips.

She softened against him.

He lowered his lips, closer and closer. They brushed lightly against hers, then they firmed, then they parted, and the kiss sent bolts of pleasure ricocheting through her.

She gripped his shoulders to steady herself. A rational part of her brain told her to stop. But she was beyond stopping. She was beyond caring about anything but the cataclysmic kiss between them.

It was Matt who finally pulled back.

He looked as dazed as she felt, and he blew out a breath. "I'm..." He gave his head a little shake. "I don't know what to say."

She forced herself to step back. "Don't." She had no

idea what to say either. "Don't try. It was just…something…that happened."

"It was something," he said.

"It was a mistake."

He raked a hand through his short hair. "It sure wasn't on purpose."

"We should get going," she said, anxious to focus on something else.

The last thing she wanted to do was dissect their kiss. The last thing she wanted to do was admit how it impacted her. The last thing she wanted her boss to know was that she saw him as a man, more than a boss.

She couldn't do that. She had to stop doing it. In this relationship, she was a mechanic, not a woman.

"We're not going anywhere." He looked pointedly out the window where the rain was driving down.

Tasha took note of the pitching floor beneath her.

It was Matt who reached for the marine radio and turned the dial to get a weather report.

"We might as well grab something to eat," he said. "This could last awhile."

Two

Waiting out the storm, Matt had fallen asleep in the living area. He awoke four hours later to find Tasha gone, and he went looking.

The yacht was rocking up and down on six-foot swells, and rain clattered against the windows. He couldn't find her on the upper decks, so he took the narrow staircase, making his way to the engine and mechanical rooms. Sure enough, he found her there. She'd removed the front panel of the generator and was elbow deep in the mechanics.

"What are you doing?" he asked.

She tensed at the sound of his voice. She was obviously remembering their kiss. Well, he remembered it, too, and it sure made him tense up. Partly because he was her boss and he felt guilty for letting things get out of hand. But partly because it had been such an amazing kiss and he desperately wanted to do it again.

"Maintenance," she answered him without turning.

He settled his shoulder against the doorjamb. "Can you elaborate?"

"I inspected the electric and serviced the batteries.

Some of the battery connections needed cleaning. Hoses and belts all look good in here. But it was worth changing the oil filter."

"I thought you would sleep."

This was above and beyond the call of duty for anyone. He'd known Tasha was a dedicated employee, but this trip was teaching him she was one in a million.

She finally turned to face him. "I did sleep. Then I woke up."

She'd found a pair of coveralls somewhere. They were miles too big, but she'd rolled up the sleeves and the pant legs. A woman shouldn't look sexy with a wrench in her hand, a smudge of oil on her cheek, swimming in a shapeless steel gray sack.

But this one did. And he wanted to do a whole lot more than kiss her. He mentally shook away the feelings.

"If it was me—" he tried to lighten the mood and put her at ease "—I think I might have inspected the liquor cabinet."

She smiled for the briefest of seconds. "Lucky your employees aren't like you."

The smile warmed him. It turned him on, but it also made him happy.

"True enough," he said. "But there is a nice cognac in there. Perfect to have on a rainy afternoon." He could picture them doing just that.

Instead of answering, she returned to work.

He watched for a few minutes, struggling with his feelings, knowing he had to put their relationship back on an even keel.

Work—he needed to say something about work instead of sharing a cozy drink.

"Are you trying to impress me?" he asked.

She didn't pause. "Yes."

"I'm impressed."

"Good."

"You should stop working."

"I'm not finished."

"You're making me feel guilty."

She looked his way and rolled her eyes. "I'm not trying to make you feel guilty."

"Then what?"

"The maintenance needed doing. I was here. There was an opportunity."

He fought an urge to close the space between them. "Are you always like this?"

"Like what?"

"I don't know, überindustrious?"

"You say that like it's a bad thing."

He did move closer. He shouldn't, couldn't, *wouldn't* bring up their kiss. But he desperately wanted to bring it up, discuss it, dissect it, relive it. How did she feel about it now? Was she angry? Was there a chance in the world she wanted to do it again?

"It's an unnerving thing," he said.

"Then, you're very easily unnerved."

He couldn't help but smile at her comeback. "I'm trying to figure you out."

"Well, that's a waste of time."

"I realize I don't know you well."

"You don't need to know me well. Just sign my paycheck."

Well, that was a crystal clear signal. He was her boss, nothing more. He swallowed his disappointment.

Then again, if he was her boss, he was her boss. He reached forward to take the wrench from her hand. "It's after five and it's a Saturday and you're done."

Their fingers touched. Stupid mistake. He felt a current run up the center of his arm.

Her grip tightened on the wrench as she tried to tug it from his grasp. "Let it go."

"It's time to clock out."

"Seriously, Matt. I'm not done yet."

His hand wrapped around hers, and his feet took him closer still.

"Matt." There was a warning in her voice, but then their gazes caught and held.

Her eyes turned moss green, deep and yielding. She was feeling something. She had to be feeling something.

She used her free hand to grasp his arm. Her grip was strong, stronger than he'd imagined. He liked that.

"We can't do this, Matt."

"I know."

She swallowed, and her voice seemed strained. "So let go."

"I want to kiss you again."

"It's a bad idea."

"You're right." His disappointment was acute. "It is."

She didn't step back, and her lips parted as she drew in a breath. "We need to keep it simple, straightforward."

"Why?"

"The signature on my paycheck."

"Is that the only reason?" It was valid. But he was curious. He was intensely curious.

"I'm not that kind of girl."

He knew she didn't mean to be funny, but he couldn't help but joke. "The kind that kisses men?"

"The kind that randomly kisses my boss—or any coworker for that matter—while I'm working, in an engine room, covered in grease."

"That's fair."

"You bet, it's fair. Not that I need your approval. Now, let go of my hand."

He glanced down, realizing they were still touching. The last thing he wanted to do was let her go. But he had no choice.

She set down the wrench, replacing it with a screwdriver. Then she lifted the generator panel and put it in place.

He moved away and braced a hand on a crossbeam above his head. "The storm's letting up."

"Good." The word sounded final. Matt didn't want it to be final.

He was her boss, sure. He understood that was a complication. But did it have to be a deal breaker? But he wanted to get to know her. He'd barely scratched the surface, and he liked her a lot.

They'd brought *Orca's Run* back to the marina, arriving late in the evening.

Tasha had spent the night and half of today attempting to purge Matt's kiss from her mind. It wasn't working. She kept reliving the pleasure, then asking herself what it all meant.

She didn't even know how she felt, never mind how Matt felt. He was a smooth-talking, great-looking man who, from everything she'd seen, could have any woman in the world. What could possibly be his interest in her?

Okay, maybe if she'd taken her mother's advice, maybe if she'd acted like a woman, dressed like a woman and got a different job, maybe then it would make sense for Matt to be interested. Matt reminded her so much of the guys she'd known in Boston, the ones who'd dated her sisters and attended all the parties.

They'd all wanted women who were super feminine. They'd been amused by Tasha. She wasn't a buddy and she wasn't, in their minds, a woman worth pursuing. She hadn't fit in anywhere. It was the reason she'd left. And now Matt was confusing her. She hated being confused.

So, right now, this afternoon, she had a new focus.

Since she'd been promoted, she had to replace herself. Matt employed several general dock laborers who also worked as mechanical assistants, and they pulled in mechanical specialists when necessary. But one staff mechanic couldn't keep up with the workload at Whiskey Bay. Matt owned twenty-four boats in all, ranging from *Monty's Pride* right down to a seventeen-foot runabout they used in the bay. Some were workboats, but most were pleasure craft available for rental.

Cash flow was a definite issue, especially after Matt's divorce. It was more important than ever that the yachts stay in good working order to maximize rentals.

Tasha was using a vacant office in the main marina building at the edge of the company pier. The place was a sprawling, utilitarian building, first constructed in 1970, with major additions built in 2000 and 2010. Its clay-colored steel siding protected against the wind and salt water.

Inside, the client area was nicely decorated, as were Matt's and the sales manager's offices. But down the hall, where the offices connected to the utility areas and eventually to the boat garage and the small dry dock, the finishing was more Spartan. Even still, she felt pretentious sitting behind a wooden desk with a guest chair in front.

She'd been through four applicants so far. One and two were nonstarters. They were handymen rather than certified marine mechanics. The third one had his certification, but something about him made Tasha cautious. He was a little too eager to list his accomplishments. He was beyond self-confident, bordering on arrogant. She didn't see him fitting in at Whiskey Bay.

The fourth applicant had been five minutes late. Not a promising start.

But then a woman appeared in the doorway. "My apologies," she said in a rush as she entered.

Tasha stood. "Alex Dumont?"

"Yes." The woman smiled broadly as she moved forward, holding out her hand.

Tasha shook it, laughing at herself for having made the assumption that Alex was a man.

"Alexandria," the woman elaborated, her eyes sparkling with humor.

"Of all people, I shouldn't make gender assumptions."

"It happens so often, I don't even think about it."

"I hear you," Tasha said. "Please, sit down."

"At least with the name Tasha nobody makes that mistake." Alex settled into the chair. "Though I have to imagine you've been written off a few times before they even met you."

"I'm not sure which is worse," Tasha said.

"I prefer the surprise value. That's why I shortened my name. I have to say this is the first time I've been interviewed by a woman."

Alex was tall, probably about five foot eight. She had wispy, wheat-blond hair, a few freckles and a pretty smile. If Tasha hadn't seen her résumé, she would have guessed she was younger than twenty-five.

"You're moving from Chicago?" Tasha asked, flipping through the three pages of Alex's résumé.

"I've already moved, three weeks ago."

"Any particular reason?" Tasha was hoping for someone who would stay in Whiskey Bay for the long term.

"I've always loved the West Coast. But mostly, it was time to make a break from the family."

Tasha could relate to that. "They didn't support your career choice?" she guessed.

"No." Alex gave a little laugh. "Quite the opposite. My father and two brothers are mechanics. They wouldn't leave me alone."

"Did you work with them?"

"At first. Then I got a job with another company. It didn't help. They still interrogated me every night and gave me advice on whatever repair I was undertaking."

"You lived with them?"

"Not anymore."

Tasha couldn't help contrasting their experiences. "I grew up in Boston. My parents wanted me to find a nice doctor or lawyer and become a wife instead of a mechanic. Though they probably would have settled for me being a landscape painter or a dancer."

"Any brothers and sisters?"

"Two sisters. Both married to lawyers." Tasha didn't like to dwell on her family. It had been a long time since she'd spoken to them. She stopped herself now, and went back to Alex's résumé. "At Schneider Marine, you worked on both gas and diesel engines?"

"Yes. Gas, anywhere from 120-horse outboards and up, and diesel, up to 550."

"Any experience on Broadmores?"

"Oh, yeah. Finicky buggers, those."

"We have two of them."

"Well, I've got their number."

Tasha couldn't help but smile. This was the kind of confidence she liked. "And you went to Riverside Tech?"

"I did. I finished my apprenticeship four years ago. I can get you a copy of my transcript if you need it."

Tasha shook her head. "I'm more interested in your recent experience. How much time on gasoline engines versus diesel?"

"More diesel, maybe seventy-five/twenty-five. Lots of service, plenty of rebuilds."

"Diagnostics?"

"I was their youngest mechanic, so I wasn't afraid of the new scan tools."

"You dive right in?" Tasha was liking Alex more and more as the interview went on.

"I dive right in."

"When can you start?"

Alex grinned. "Can you give me a few days to unpack?"

"Absolutely."

Both women came to their feet.

"Then, I'm in," Alex said.

Tasha shook her hand, excited at the prospect of another female mechanic in the company. "Welcome aboard."

Alex left, but a few minutes later, Tasha was still smiling when Matt came through the door.

"What?" he asked.

"What?" she returned, forcibly dampening her exhilaration at the sight of him.

She couldn't do this. She *wouldn't* do this. They had an employer-employee relationship, not a man-woman relationship.

"You're smiling," he said.

"I'm happy."

"About what?"

"I love my job."

"Is that all?"

"You don't think I love my job?" She did love it.

And she had a feeling she'd love it even more with Alex around.

"I was hoping you were happy to see me."

"Matt." She put a warning in her voice.

"Are we going to just ignore it?"

She quickly closed the door to make sure nobody could overhear. "Yes, we're going to ignore it."

"By *it*, I mean our kiss."

She folded her arms over her chest and gave him a glare. "I know what you mean."

"Just checking," he said, looking dejected.

"Stop." She wasn't going to be emotionally manipulated.

"I'm not going to pretend. I miss you."

"There's nothing to miss. I'm right here."

"Prepared to talk work and only work."

"Yes."

He was silent for a moment. "Fine. Okay. I'll take it."

"Good." She knew with absolute certainty that it was for the best.

He squared his shoulders. "Who was that leaving?"

"That was Alex Dumont. She's our new mechanic."

Matt's brows went up. "We have a new mechanic?"

"You knew I was hiring one."

"But..."

Tasha couldn't help an inward sigh. She'd seen this reaction before. "But...she's a woman."

"That's not what I was going to say. I was surprised, is all."

"That she was light on testosterone?"

"You keep putting words in my mouth."

"Well, you keep putting expressions in your eyes."

He opened his mouth, but then he seemed to think better of whatever he'd planned to say.

"What?" she asked before she could stop herself.

"Nothing." He took a backward step. "I'm backing off. This is me backing off."

"From who I hire?"

Matt focused in on her eyes. His eyes smoldered, and she felt desire arc between them.

"I can feel it from here," he said, as if he was reading her mind.

Her brain stumbled. "There's…uh… I'm…"

"You can't quite spit out the lie, can you?"

She couldn't. Lying wouldn't help. "We have to ignore it."

"Why?"

"We do. We do, Matt."

There was a long beat of silence.

"I have a date Saturday night," he said.

A pain crossed her chest, but she steeled herself. "No kidding."

"I don't date that much."

"I don't pay any attention."

It was a lie. From the staff quarters, she'd seen him leave his house on the hill on many occasions, dressed to the nines. She'd often wondered where he'd gone, whom he'd been with, how late he'd come home.

And she'd watched him bring women to his house. They often dined on the deck. Caterers would set up candles and white linens, and then Matt and his date would chat and laugh the evening away.

She'd paid attention all right. But wild horses wouldn't drag the admission out of her.

So Saturday night, Matt had picked up the tall, willowy, expensively coiffed Emilie and brought her home for arctic char and risotto, catered by a local chef. They were dining in his glass-walled living room to candlelight and a full moon. The wine was from the Napa Valley, and the chocolate truffles were handcrafted with Belgian chocolate.

It should have been perfect. Emilie was a real estate company manager, intelligent, gracious, even a little bit funny. She was friendly and flirtatious, and made no secret of the fact that she expected a very romantic conclusion to the evening.

But Matt's gaze kept straying to the pier below, to the yachts, the office building and the repair shop. Finally, Tasha appeared. She strode briskly beneath the overhead lights, through the security gate and up the stairway that led to the staff quarters. Some of his staff members had families and houses in town. The younger, single crew members, especially those who had moved to Whiskey Bay to work at the marina, seemed to appreciate the free rent, even if the staff units were small and basic. He was happy at the moment that Tasha was one of them.

He reflexively glanced at his watch. It was nearly ten o'clock. Even for Tasha, this was late.

"Matt?" Emilie said.

"Yes?" He quickly returned his attention to her.

She gave a very pretty smile. "I asked if they were all yours?"

"All what?"

"The boats. Do you really own that many boats?"

"I do," he said. He'd told this story a hundred times. "I started with three about a decade ago. Business was good, so I gradually added to the fleet."

He glanced back to the pier, but Tasha had disappeared from view. He told himself not to be disappointed. He'd see her again soon. It had been a few days now since they'd run into each other. He'd tried not to miss her, but he did. He'd find a reason to talk to her tomorrow.

Emilie pointed toward the window. "That one is *huge*."

"*Monty's Pride* is our largest vessel."

"Could I see the inside?" she asked, eyes alight. "Would you give me a tour?"

Before Matt could answer, there was a pounding on his door.

"Expecting someone?" she asked, looking a little bit frustrated by the interruption.

His friends and neighbors, Caleb Watford and TJ Bauer, were the only people who routinely dropped by. But neither of them would knock. At most, they'd call out from the entryway if they thought they might walk in on something.

Matt rose. "I'll be right back."

"Sure." Emilie helped herself to another truffle. "I'll wait here."

The date had been going pretty well so far. But Matt couldn't say he was thrilled with the touch of sarcasm he'd just heard in Emilie's voice.

The knock came again as he got to the front entry. He swung open the door.

Tasha stood on his porch, her work jacket wrinkled, a blue baseball cap snug on her head and her work boots sturdy against the cool weather.

His immediate reaction was delight. He wanted to drag her inside and make her stay for a while.

"What's up?" he asked instead, remembering the promise he'd made, holding himself firmly at a respectful distance.

"Something's going on," she said.

"Between us?" he asked before he could stop himself,

resisting the urge to glance back and be sure Emilie was still out of sight.

Tasha frowned. "*No.* With *Pacific Wind.*" She named the single-engine twenty-eight-footer. "It's just a feeling. But I'm worried."

He stepped back and gestured for her to come inside.

She glanced down at her boots.

"Don't worry about it," he said. "I have a cleaning service."

"A cable broke on the steering system," she said.

"Is that a major problem?"

He didn't particularly care why she'd decided to come up and tell him in person. He was just glad she had.

It was the first time she'd been inside his house. He couldn't help but wonder if she liked the modern styling, the way it jutted out from the hillside, the clean lines, glass walls and unobstructed view. He really wanted to find out. He hadn't been interested in Emilie's opinion, but he was curious about Tasha's.

"It's not a big problem," she said. "I fixed it. It's fixed."

"That's good." He dared to hope all over again that this was a personal visit disguised as business.

"Matt?" came Emilie's voice.

He realized he'd forgotten all about her.

"I'll just be a minute," he called back to her.

"You're busy," Tasha said, looking instantly regretful. "Of course you're busy. I didn't think." She glanced at her watch. "This is Saturday, isn't it?"

"You forgot the day of the week?"

"Matt, honey." Emilie came up behind him.

Honey? Seriously? After a single date?

Not even a single date, really. The date hadn't concluded yet.

"Who's this?" Emilie asked.

There was a dismissive edge to her voice and judgment in her expression as she gave Tasha the once-over, clearly finding her lacking.

The superior attitude annoyed Matt. “This is Tasha.”

“I’m the mechanic,” Tasha said, not seeming remotely bothered by Emilie’s condescension.

“Hmph,” Emilie said, wrinkling her perfect nose. She wrapped her arm possessively through Matt’s. “Is this an emergency?”

Tasha took a step back, opening her mouth to speak.

“Yes,” Matt said. “It’s an emergency. I’m afraid I’m going to have to cut our date short.”

He wasn’t sure who looked more surprised by his words, Emilie or Tasha.

“I’ll call you a ride.” He took out his phone.

It took Emilie a moment to find her voice. “What *kind* of emergency?”

“The mechanical kind,” he said flatly, suddenly tired of her company.

He typed in the request. He definitely didn’t want Tasha to leave.

“But—” Emilie began.

“The ride will be here in three minutes,” he said. “I’ll get your coat.”

He did a quick check of Tasha’s expression, steeling himself for the possibility that she’d speak up and out him as a liar.

She didn’t.

He quickly retrieved Emilie’s coat and purse.

“I don’t mind waiting,” Emilie said, a plaintive whine in her voice.

“I couldn’t ask you to do that.” He held up the coat.

“How long do you think—”

"Could be a long time. It could be a very long time. It's complicated."

"Matt, I can—" Tasha began.

"No. Nope." He gave a definitive shake to his head. "It's business. It's important." It might not be critical, but Tasha had never sought him out after hours before, so there had to be something going on.

"You're a *mechanic*?" Emilie asked Tasha.

"A marine mechanic."

"So you get all greasy and stuff?"

"Sometimes."

"That must be awful." Emilie gave a little shudder.

"Emilie." Matt put a warning tone in his voice.

She crooked her head back to look at him. "What? It's weird."

"It's not weird."

"It's unusual," Tasha said. "But women are up to nearly fifteen percent in the mechanical trades, higher when you look at statistics for those of us under thirty-five."

Emilie didn't seem to know what to say in response.

Matt's phone pinged.

"Your ride's here," he told Emilie, ushering her toward the door.

Tasha stood to one side, and he watched until Emilie got into the car.

"You didn't have to do that," Tasha said as he closed the door.

"It wasn't going well."

"In that case, I'm happy to be your wingman."

Matt zeroed in on her expression to see if she was joking. She looked serious, and he didn't like the sound of that.

"I don't need a wingman."

"Tell me what's going on." He gestured through the archway to the living room.

She crouched down to untie her boots.

"You don't have to—"

"Your carpet is white," she said.

"I suppose."

Most of the women he brought home wore delicate shoes, stiletto heels and such.

Tasha peeled off her boots, revealing thick wool socks. For some reason, the sight made him smile.

She rose, looking all business.

"Care for a drink?" he asked, gesturing her forward.

She moved, shooting him an expression of disbelief on the way past. "No, I don't want a drink."

"I opened a great bottle of pinot noir. I'm not going to finish it myself."

"This isn't a social visit," she said, glancing around the room at the pale white leather furniture and long, narrow gas fireplace.

She was obviously hesitant to sit down in her work clothes.

"Here," he suggested, pointing to the formal dining room. The chairs were dark oak, likely less intimidating if she was worried about leaving dirt on anything.

While she sat down, he retrieved the pinot from the glass porch and brought two fresh glasses.

He sat down cornerwise to her and set down the wine.

She gave him an exaggerated sigh. "I'm not drinking while I work."

"It's ten o'clock on a Saturday night."

"Your point?"

"My point is you're officially off the clock."

"So, you're not paying me?"

"I'll pay you anything you want." He poured them each some of the rich, dark wine. "Aren't you on salary?"

"I am."

"You work an awful lot of overtime."

"A good deal for you."

"I'm giving you a raise." He held one of the glasses out for her.

"Ha ha," she mocked.

"Take it," he said.

She did, but set it down on the table in front of her.

"Twenty percent," he told her.

"You can't do that."

"I absolutely can." He raised his glass. "Let's toast your raise."

"I came here to tell you I might have made a big mistake."

Three

Tasha reluctantly took a sip of the wine, noting right away that it was a fantastic vintage. She looked at the bottle, recognizing the Palmer Valley label as one of her parents' favorites, and the Crispin Pinot Noir as one of their higher-end brands.

"You have good taste in wine," she said.

"I'm glad you like it."

His smile was warm, and she felt an unwelcome glow in the pit of her stomach.

To distract herself, she tipped the bottle to check the year.

"You know the label?" he asked, sounding surprised.

"Mechanics can't appreciate fine wine?"

He paused to take in her expression. "Clearly, they can."

It was annoying how his deep voice strummed along her nervous system. She seemed to have no defenses against him.

She set down her glass and straightened in her chair, reminding herself this was business.

"What did I say?" he asked.

"I came here to tell you—"

"I just said something wrong," he persisted. "What was it?"

"You didn't say anything wrong." It was her problem, not his. "*Pacific Wind* broke down near Granite Point."

"Another breakdown?"

"Like I said, a cable was broken."

"But you fixed it." He slid the wineglass a little closer to her. "Good job. Well done, you."

"It shouldn't have happened. I serviced it just last week. I must have missed a weak point."

His lips tightened in what looked like frustration. "Why are you so quick to blame yourself? It obviously broke *after* you did your work."

"The sequence of events isn't logical. It shouldn't have broken all of a sudden. Wear and tear should have been obvious when I was working on it." She'd been mulling over the possibilities for hours now. "It could have been a faulty part, weak material in the cable maybe, something that wasn't visible that would leave it prone to breaking."

"There you go."

"Or…" She hesitated to even voice her speculation.

"Or?" he prompted.

"Somebody wanted it to break. It's far-fetched. I get that. And on the surface, it seems like I'm making excuses for my own incompetence—coming up with some grand scheme of sabotage to explain it all away. But the thing is, I checked with the fuel supply company right after we got back from Tyree. We were the only customer that had a water problem. And none of our other yachts were affected, only *Orca's Run*. How does that work? How does water only get into one fuel system?" She gave in and took another drink of the wine.

"Tasha?" Matt asked.

"Yeah?" She set down her glass, oddly relieved at having said it out loud. Now they could discuss it and dismiss it.

"Can you parse that out a little more for me?"

She nodded, happy to delve into her theory and find the flaws. "It's far from definitive. It's only possible. It's possible that someone put water in the fuel and damaged the pump. And it's possible someone partially cut the cable."

"The question is, why?"

She agreed. "Do you have any enemies?"

"None that I know about."

"A competitor, maybe?"

He sat back in his chair. "Wow."

"*Wow* that somebody could be secretly working against you?"

"No. I was just thinking that after-dinner conversation with you is *so* much more interesting than with Emilie."

"So you think my theory is too far-fetched." She was inclined to agree.

"That's not what I said at all. I'm thinking you could be right. And we should investigate. And that's kind of exciting."

"You think it's exciting? That someone might be damaging your boats and undermining your company's reputation?"

He topped up both of their glasses. "I think it could be exciting to investigate. It's not like anything was seriously or permanently damaged. It seems like more mischief than anything. And haven't you ever wanted to be an amateur sleuth?"

"No." She could honestly say it had never crossed her mind.

"Come on. You investigate, diagnose and fix problems all the time."

"There are no bad guys lurking inside engines."

"The bad guy only adds a new dimension to the problem."

She couldn't understand his jovial attitude. There wasn't a positive side to this. "There's something wrong with you, Matt."

"Will you help me?" he asked, his eyes alight in a way that trapped and held her gaze. His eyes were vivid blue right now, the color of the bay at a summer sunrise.

"It's my job." She fought an inappropriate thrill at the prospect of working closely with him. She should be staying away from him. That's what she should be doing.

"We need to start with a list of suspects. Who has access to the engines and steering systems?"

"I do, and the contract mechanics from Dean's Repairs and Corner Service. And Alex now. But she wasn't even here when we had the *Orca's Run* problem."

"Was she in Whiskey Bay?"

"Yes but… You're not suggesting she's a mole."

"I'm not suggesting anything yet. I'm only laying out the facts."

Tasha didn't want to suspect Alex, but she couldn't disagree with Matt's approach. They had to start with everyone who had access, especially those with mechanical skills. Whoever did this understood boats and engines well enough to at least attempt to cover their tracks.

"At least we can rule you out," Matt said with a smirk.

"And you," she returned.

"And me. What about the rest of the staff? Who can we rule out?"

"Can we get a list of everyone's hours for the past couple of weeks?"

"Easily."

"What about your competitors?" It seemed to Tasha that Matt's competitors would have motive to see him fail.

"They'd have a financial motive, I suppose. But I know most of the ones in the area, and I can't imagine any of them doing something underhanded."

"Maybe they didn't," she said, realizing the enormity of her accusations. Never mind the enormity, what about the likelihood that somebody was out to harm Matt's business?

She was reevaluating this whole thing. "Maybe it was just my making a mistake."

He paused and seemed to consider. "Do you believe that's what happened?"

"Nobody's perfect." She knew her negligence could account for the cable.

Then again, the water in the fuel of *Orca's Run* was something else. It was a lot less likely she'd been responsible for that.

He watched her closely, his gaze penetrating. "Tasha, I can tell by your expression you know it wasn't you."

"I can't be one hundred percent certain."

He took her hand in both of his. "I am."

Their gazes met and held, and the air temperature in the room seemed to rise. Subtle sounds magnified: the wind, the surf, the hiss of the fireplace. Heat rushed up her arm, blooming into desire in her chest.

Like the first rumblings of an earthquake, she could feel it starting all over again.

"I have to go." She jumped to her feet.

He stood with her, still holding her hand. His gaze moved to her lips.

They tingled.

She knew she should move. She needed to move *right now.*

She did move. But it was to step forward, not backward.

She brought her free hand up to his. He interlaced their fingers.

"Tasha," he whispered.

She should run. Leave. But instead she let her eyes drift closed. She leaned in, crossing the last few inches between them. She tipped her chin, tilted her head. She might not have a lot of experience with romance, but she knew she was asking for his kiss.

He didn't disappoint.

With a swift, indrawn breath, he brought his lips to hers.

The kiss was tender, soft and tentative. But it sent waves through her body, heat and energy. It was she who pressed harder, she who parted her lips and she who disentangled her hands to wrap her arms around his neck.

He gave a small groan, and he embraced her, his solid forearms against her back, pressing her curves against the length of his body, thigh to thigh, chest to chest. Her nipples peaked at his touch, the heat of his skin. She desperately wanted to feel his skin against hers. But she'd retained just enough sanity to stop herself.

The kiss was as far as it could go.

She reluctantly drew back. She wished she could look away and pretend it hadn't happened. But she didn't. She wouldn't. She faced him head-on.

His eyes were opaque, and there was a ghost of a smile on his face.

"You're amazing," he said.

"We can't do that." Regret was pouring in, along with a healthy dose of self-recrimination.

"But, we do."

"You know what I mean."

"You mean *shouldn't*." His closeness was still clouding her mind.

"Yes, shouldn't. No, can't. You have to help me here, Matt." She stepped away, putting some space between them.

He gave an exaggerated sigh. "You're asking a lot."

She wanted to be honest, and she wanted both of them to be realistic. "I like it here."

He glanced around his living room that jutted out from the cliff, affording incredible views of the bay. He was clearly proud of the design, proud of his home. "I'm glad to hear that."

"Not the house," she quickly corrected him.

"You don't like my house?"

"That's not what I mean. I do like your house." The house was stunningly gorgeous; anyone would love it. "I mean I like working at Whiskey Bay. I don't want to have to quit."

His expression turned to incredulity. "You're making some pretty huge leaps in logic."

She knew that was true, and she backpedaled. "I'm not assuming you want a fling."

"That's not what I—"

"It's hard for a woman to be taken seriously as a mechanic."

"So you've said."

"I want to keep my personal life and my professional life separate."

"Everybody does. Until something happens that makes them want something else."

Now she just wanted out of this conversation. "I'm afraid I've given you the wrong idea."

"The only idea you've given me is that you're attracted to me."

She wanted to protest, but she wasn't going to lie.

He continued. "That and the fact that you believe my company is the target of sabotage."

She quickly latched onto the alternative subject. "I do. At least, it's a possibility that we should consider."

"And I trust your judgment, so we're going to investigate."

Tasha drew a breath of relief. They were back on solid ground. All work with Matt, no play. That was her mission going forward.

Matt couldn't concentrate on work. He kept reliving his kiss with Tasha over and over again.

He was with TJ and Caleb on the top deck of his marina building, standing around the propane fireplace as the sun sank into the Pacific. The other men's voices were more a drone of noise than a conversation.

"Why would anyone sabotage your engines?" TJ broke through Matt's daydreaming.

"What?" he asked, shaking himself back to the present.

"Why would they do it?"

"Competition is my guess." Matt hadn't been able to come up with another reason.

Caleb levered into one of the padded deck chairs. It was a cool evening, but the men still sipped on chilled beers.

"What about your surveillance cameras?" Caleb asked.

"Not enough of them to provide full coverage. They're pretty easy to avoid if that's your intention."

"You should get more."

"I've ordered more." It was one of the first moves Matt had made. He took a chair himself.

"Did you call the police?" TJ asked, sitting down.

"Not yet. I can't imagine it would be a priority for them. And I want to make sure we're right before I waste anybody's time."

"So, Tasha is wrong?"

Matt found himself bristling at what was only the slightest of criticisms of Tasha. "No, she's not wrong."

"I'm just asking," TJ said, obviously catching the tone in Matt's voice.

"And I'm just answering. She's not one hundred percent convinced yet either. So, we'll wait."

"Until it happens again?" Caleb asked. "What if it's more serious this time? What if whoever it is targets more than the marina?"

"Are you worried about the Crab Shack?" Matt hadn't thought about the other businesses in the area, including the Crab Shack restaurant run by Caleb's new wife, Jules, who was five months pregnant with twins.

"Not yet." Caleb seemed to further contemplate the question. "I might ask Noah to spend a little more time over there."

"Nobody's going to mess with Noah," TJ said.

"He's scrappy," Caleb agreed.

Caleb's sister-in-law's boyfriend had spent a short time in jail after a fistfight in self-defense. He was tough and no-nonsense, and he'd protect Jules and her sister, Melissa, against anything and anyone.

"What about your security cameras at the Crab Shack?" TJ asked Caleb. "Would any of them reach this far?"

"I'll check," Caleb said. "But I doubt the resolution is high enough to be of any help."

"I'd appreciate that," Matt said to Caleb.

It hadn't occurred to him to worry about Tasha's or

anyone else's safety. But maybe Caleb was onto something. Maybe Matt should take a few precautions. So far, the incidents had been minor, and nobody had come close to being hurt. But that wasn't to say it couldn't happen. The incidents could escalate.

"Matt?" It was Tasha's voice coming from the pier below, and he felt the timbre radiate through his chest.

He swiftly rose and crossed to the rail, where he could see her. "Are you okay?"

She seemed puzzled by his concern. "I'm fine."

"Good."

"*Never Fear* and *Crystal Zone* are both ready to go in the morning. I'm heading into town for a few hours."

"What for?" The question was out of Matt's mouth before he realized it was none of his business. It was after five, and Tasha was free to do anything she wanted.

"Meeting some guys."

Guys? What did she mean *guys*? He wanted to ask if it was one particular guy, or if it was a group of guys. Were they all just friends?

"Hey, Tasha." TJ appeared at the rail beside him.

"Hi, TJ." Her greeting was casual, and her attention went back to Matt. "Alex will fill the fuel tanks first thing. The clients are expected at ten."

"Got it," Matt said, wishing he could ask more questions about her evening. Or better still, invite her to join them, where they could talk and laugh together.

Not that they were in the habit of friendly conversation. Mostly, they debated. But he'd be happy to engage her in a rollicking debate about pretty much any subject.

As she walked away, TJ spoke up. "I may just take another shot."

"Another shot at what?" Matt asked.

"At your mechanic."

"What?" Matt turned.

"I like her."

"What do you mean *another* shot?" Matt was surprised by the level of his anger. "You took a shot at her already?"

TJ was obviously taken aback by Matt's reaction. "I asked you back in the summer. You told me to go for it."

"That was months ago."

"That's when I asked her out. I suggested dinner and dancing. That might have been my mistake."

Matt took a drink of his beer to keep himself from saying anything more. He didn't like the thought of Tasha with any guy, never mind TJ. TJ was the epitome of rich, good-looking and eligible. Matt had seen the way a lot of women reacted to him. Not that Tasha was an ordinary woman. Still, she was a woman.

TJ kept talking, half to himself. "Maybe a monster truck rally? She is a mechanic."

Caleb joined them at the rail.

TJ tried again. "Maybe an auto show. There's one coming up in Seattle."

"You can't ask her out," Matt said.

The protest caught Caleb's attention. "Why can't he ask her out?"

"Because she's already turned him down."

"I could be persistent," TJ said.

"I really don't think dinner and dancing or persistence was the problem," Matt said.

"How would you know that?" TJ asked.

Caleb's expression took a speculative turn. "You have a problem with TJ asking Tasha out?"

"No," Matt responded to Caleb. Then he reconsidered his answer. "Yes."

TJ leaned an elbow on the rail, a grin forming on his face. "Oh, this is interesting."

"It's not interesting," Matt said.

"Is something going on between you two?" Caleb asked.

"No. Nothing is going on."

"But you like her." TJ's grin was full-on now.

"I kissed her. She kissed me. We kissed." Matt wasn't proud that it sounded like he was bragging. "She's a nice woman. And I like her. But nothing has happened."

"Are you telling me to back off?" TJ asked.

"That's pretty loud and clear," Caleb said.

TJ held up his hands in mock surrender. "Backing off."

"She said she was meeting a guy tonight?" Caleb raised a brow.

Matt narrowed his gaze. "She said *guys*, plural. They're probably just friends of hers."

"Probably," said TJ with exaggerated skepticism, still clearly amused at Matt's expense.

"It took you long enough," Caleb said.

"There is no *it*," Matt responded. It had taken him too long to notice her. He'd own that.

"Have you asked her out?"

"We're a little busy at the moment. You know, distracted by criminal activity."

"That's a no," TJ said. "At least I took the plunge."

"You got shot down," Caleb reminded TJ.

"No risk, no reward."

"She's gun-shy," Matt said. He didn't know what made her that way, but it was obvious she was wary of dating.

"So, what are you going to do?" Caleb asked.

"Nothing."

"That's a mistake."

"I'm not going to force anything." The last thing Matt

wanted to do was make Tasha feel uncomfortable working at the marina.

He wanted her to stay. For all kinds of different reasons, both personal and professional, but he definitely wanted her to stay.

The Edge Bar and Grill in the town of Whiskey Bay was a popular hangout for the marina staff. It also drew in the working class from the local service and supply businesses. The artsy crowd preferred the Blue Badger on Third Avenue. While those who were looking for something high-end and refined could choose the Ocean View Lounge across the highway. While the Crab Shack was becoming popular, drawing people from the surrounding towns and even as far away as Olympia.

Tasha liked the Edge. The decor was particularly attractive tonight, decked out for the season with a tree, lights and miles of evergreen garlands. A huge wreath over the bar was covered in gold balls and poinsettia flowers.

As was usual, the music had a rock-and-country flare. The menu was unpretentious. They had good beer on tap, and soda refills were free. She was driving hcr and Alex home tonight, so she'd gone with cola.

"Have you heard of anybody having any unexpected engine problems lately?" she asked Henry Schneider, who was sitting across the table.

Henry was a marine mechanic at Shutters Corner ten miles down the highway near the public wharf.

"Unexpected how?" he asked.

"We had some water in the fuel with no apparent cause."

"Loose cap?"

"Checked that, along with the fuel source. The water separator was full."

"There's your problem."

"I swapped it out, but I couldn't figure out how it got that way."

Henry gave a shrug. "It happens."

Alex returned from the small dance floor with another mechanic, James Hamilton, in tow.

"So, no reports of anything strange?" Tasha asked Henry.

"Strange?" James asked, helping Alex onto the high stool.

"Unexplained mechanical failures in the area."

"There's always an explanation," James said. "Sometimes you just have to keep looking."

"You want to dance?" Alex asked Henry.

"Who says I was through dancing?" James asked her.

"Dance with Tasha." Alex motioned for Henry to come with her.

He swallowed the remainder of his beer and rose from his chair.

James held out his hand to Tasha.

She gave up talking shop and accepted the invitation.

James was younger than Henry, likely in his late twenties. He was from Idaho and had a fresh-faced openness about him that Tasha liked. He was tall and lanky. His hair was red, and his complexion was fair. She didn't think she'd ever seen him in a bad mood.

It wasn't the first time they'd ever danced together, and he was good at it. He'd once told her barn dancing was a popular pastime in the small town where he'd grown up. She knew he'd left his high school sweetheart behind, and she got the feeling he'd one day return to her, even if he did prefer the West Coast to rural Idaho.

As the song ended, a figure appeared behind James. It took only a split second for Tasha to recognize Matt.

"What are you doing here?" she asked him, her guard immediately going up. She assumed this was too simple, too low-key to be his kind of place. "Is something wrong?"

"Dance?" he asked instead of answering.

James backed away. "Catch you later."

Matt stepped in front of her as a Bruce Springsteen song came up.

He took her hand.

"Did something happen?" she asked. "Was there another breakdown?"

"Nothing happened. Can't a guy go out for the evening?"

She struggled to ignore his light touch on her back and the heat where his hand joined hers. It was a lost cause. "This isn't your typical hangout."

"Sure it is."

"I can tell when you're lying."

He hesitated. "I was worried about you."

"Why?"

"There's a criminal out there."

She almost laughed. "If there is, he's focused on your company. It has nothing to do with me."

"We don't know that."

"We do."

He drew her closer as they danced, even though she knew getting more intimate with Matt was a big mistake.

But the words didn't come. Instead of speaking, she followed his lead. It was the path of least resistance, since their bodies moved seamlessly together. He was tall and solid and a smooth, skilled dancer.

She told herself she could handle it. They were in public after all. It's not like they would get carried away.

"I know you like to be independent," he said.

"I am independent."

"The truth is, people are less likely to harass you if you're with me."

His words were confusing.

"Nobody's been harassing me. Nobody's going to harass me."

Matt glanced around the room with apparent skepticism, as if he was expecting a gang of criminals to be lurking next to the dance floor.

"See that guy in the red shirt?" She pointed. "He worked at Shutters Corner. And the guy talking to Alex? He's Henry's coworker. They're local guys, Matt. They're mechanics. There are a lot of local mechanics here. And I'm talking to them all."

Matt's hold on her tightened. "Are you dancing with them all?"

She tipped her chin to look up at him, seeing his lips were thin and his jaw was tight.

He looked jealous. The last thing she wanted him to be was jealous. But her heart involuntarily lifted at the idea.

"No." The sharp retort was as much for her as it was for him. "I'm here asking questions. I'm gathering evidence, if you must know."

"Oh," he drawled with immediate understanding.

"Yes, *oh*. If anybody's having the same problems as us, these guys are going to know about it."

"That's a really good idea."

She put a note of sarcasm into her tone. "Why, thank you."

"I'm not crazy about the dancing part."

"*You* asked *me*," she pointed out.

"What? No, not with me." He canted his head. "With them."

She wanted to point out that he was dating other women. But she quickly stopped herself. Matt's romantic life was none of her business. And hers was none of his. The more women he dated, the better.

His voice lowered. "You can dance with me all you want."

"We're not going there, Matt."

"Okay." His agreement was easy, but his hold still felt intimate.

"You say okay, but we're still dancing." She knew she could pull away herself. She knew she should do exactly that, but he felt so good in her arms, she wanted to hang on just a little bit longer.

"The song will be over soon." He went silent for a moment. "How are you getting home?"

"Driving."

"You came alone?"

"I drove with Alex. Matt, I've been going out at night on my own for the past six years."

"Not while my boats were being sabotaged all around you."

"We don't know that they are being sabotaged. Honestly, I'm beginning to regret sharing my suspicions with you." The last thing she'd expected was for him to go all bodyguard on her.

"We don't know that they're not. And don't you dare hold anything back."

She stopped dancing. "Matt."

His hand contracted around her shoulder. "I didn't mean for that to sound like an order."

"Is there something you're not telling me?"

Had there been some development? Was there a danger she didn't know about?

"I heard TJ ask you out."

The statement took her completely by surprise. "That was a long time ago. You can't possibly suspect TJ."

Sure, she'd turned TJ down. But he and Matt were good friends. He wouldn't take out his anger with her by harming Matt. Plus, he hadn't even seemed to care that much. He was still friendly to her.

"I *don't* suspect TJ."

The song changed to a Christmas tune. It wasn't the best dance music in the world, but Matt kept leading, so she followed.

"Then why are we talking about him?"

Matt seemed to be reviewing their conversation so far. "It was Caleb."

"You suspect Caleb?" That was even more outlandish than suspecting TJ.

"Caleb's the one who got me worried about the sabotage. He's worried about Jules, which got me to thinking about you. And then TJ mentioned that he'd asked you out."

"Caleb worries too much. And TJ was months ago."

"So, you're not interested in him?"

Tasha was more than confused here. "Did he ask you to ask me?"

One minute, she thought Matt was romancing her, and she braced herself to shut him down. And then he seemed to be TJ's wingman. Their kisses notwithstanding, maybe she was reading his interest all wrong.

Before Matt could respond, she jumped back in. "TJ's not my type."

Alex appeared beside Tasha on the dance floor.

She took Tasha's arm and leaned into her ear. "James offered me a ride home."

Tasha pulled back to look at her friend. "Is that a good thing?"

Alex's eyes were alight. "You bet."

Since Alex had a done a whole lot more dancing than drinking, Tasha wasn't worried about her. And Tasha had known James for months. He seemed like a very upstanding guy.

"Do you mind if I bail on you?" Alex asked.

"Not at all. I'll see you later."

Alex grinned. "Thanks." Her walk was light as she moved away.

"So, you're driving home alone," Matt said. "I'll follow you."

Tasha rolled her eyes at him.

"I'm serious."

"Thanks for the dance," she said and pulled back from his arms.

She was going to have another drink. She was going to chat with Henry and the other mechanics. She didn't need a bodyguard.

Four

Matt hung back as Tasha approached her compact car in the Edge's parking lot. It was in a dark corner, and he moved out of the building's lights so his eyes could adjust.

It was obvious she knew he was there, knew he'd waited for her to leave for home. She'd shot him a look of frustration as she'd headed for the front door and he'd risen from his seat at the bar.

Now, she shook her head with exaggerated resignation and gave him a mocking wave as she slipped into the driver's seat.

He didn't really care how she felt. Caleb had him worried about safety. He headed for his own car at the opposite side of the parking lot. The bar was only half-full at ten o'clock. But even on a weeknight, the crowd here would keep going until midnight, when the place shut down.

Tasha's engine cranked. Then it cranked again. But it didn't catch and start. A third crank was followed by silence.

Matt turned back.

She was out of the car and opening the hood.

"Need some help?" he asked as he approached.

She laughed. "You *have* read my résumé, right?"

"I'm not questioning your technical skills. And it's obviously a dead battery."

Her annoyance seemed to fade. "That's exactly what it is."

As they gazed at the cold engine, a thought struck him. "Could this be sabotage?"

"No." Her answer was definitive.

"How can you be sure?"

"Because it's related to my having an old battery. I've been limping it along for a while now. Do you have cables?"

"In my BMW?"

"BMWs run the same way as any other car."

"My battery's under warranty. And I have roadside assistance. You don't have cables?"

Tasha was a be-prepared kind of woman. Jumper cables seemed like the kind of thing she would carry.

She looked embarrassed. "I do. Usually. I took them out of my trunk to help Alex move her stuff."

"Come on," he said, motioning to his car.

"I'll call a tow truck and get a jump."

"There's no need." He wasn't about to leave her standing in a dark parking lot waiting for a tow truck. "I'll bring you back tomorrow with your jumper cables."

"I can take care of it."

His frustration mounted. "Why are you arguing?"

She squared her shoulders and lifted her chin but didn't answer.

"Well?" he prompted.

"I don't know."

He couldn't help but grin. "Pride?"

"Maybe. I don't like to be rescued."

"But you'll accept help from a random tow truck driver."

She dropped the hood down, and the sound echoed. "He's paid to help me. But you're right. I'm wrong. I'd appreciate the ride home."

"Did you just say I was right?"

She locked the driver's door and started walking. "I did."

He fell into step beside her. "It's fun being right."

"Calm down. It's not that exciting."

He hit the remote to unlock the doors. "You're positive somebody wasn't messing with your battery?"

"I'm positive. It's unrelated. And if we try to link it in, we'll set ourselves off in the wrong direction."

Matt thought about her logic for a moment. "Okay. Now you're the one who's right."

She cracked a smile. "Thank goodness I'm evening things up."

He opened the driver's door while she did the same on the passenger side.

"But I'm not wrong," he pointed out.

"Maybe a little bit."

"Maybe not at all. I just asked a question. Postulating something is not the same as being incorrect about it."

"You're right," she said and plunked into the seat.

He leaned down to look through his open door. "That's two for me."

She was smiling as she buckled her seat belt.

He started the engine, turned down the music and pulled out of the parking lot.

The temperature was in the fifties, but the interior heated up quickly, and Tasha unzipped her fitted gray leather jacket. She wore a purple tank top beneath it over a boxy pair of faded blue jeans and brown Western-style boots. Her hair was pulled into a high ponytail. It was mostly brunette, but it flashed with amber highlights as they drove.

She looked casual and comfortable, sexy at the same time. He liked it. He liked it a lot.

"Nobody I talked to knew anything," she said. "Nothing weird going on out there in the broader Whiskey Bay mechanical world."

"So the marina is the target."

"That would be my guess. Or it's a couple of coincidences. It could still be that."

He didn't disagree. He hoped it was a couple of coincidences. "I'm going to check out my competition."

"How?"

"'Tis the season. There are a lot of gatherings and parties coming up. The business community likes to celebrate together."

"I remember."

"Were you here last year?"

She'd been working at the marina only since March.

"I was talking about the business community anywhere. It was the same while I was growing up."

"You went to corporate Christmas parties?" He tried to picture it.

"I read about them," she continued, quickly. "They sounded...posh and snooty and boring."

He laughed at how she wrinkled her nose. "They're not bad. They are fancy. But some of the people are interesting."

She gave a derisive scoff.

"Hey, I'm one of those people. Am I that bad?"

"In some ways, yes."

"What ways?" He tried not to let her opinion get to him.

"The way you dress. The way you talk."

"What's wrong with the way I talk?"

She seemed to think about that. "It's clear and precise, with very little slang. You have a wide vocabulary."

"I'm not seeing the problem."

"It sounds posh."

"What about you?"

She was easily as articulate as him.

"I'm perfectly ordinary."

She wasn't. But he wasn't going to get into that argument right now.

"And so are the people at the corporate parties. You shouldn't be biased against them." He slowed the car and turned from the highway down his long driveway that wound through the woods.

"I can't stand those frilly, frothy dresses, those pretentious caviar and foie gras canapés, and the ceaseless conversation about who's making partner and the who's marrying who."

He wasn't about to admit she'd nailed it—at least when it came to some of the guests at those parties.

"You shouldn't knock it until you've tried it," he said instead.

"You're right."

He chuckled. "And I've hit the trifecta."

Then the headlights caught his house. He blinked to check his vision on what he thought he saw there. His stomach curled. It couldn't be.

"Who's that?" Tasha asked as the car came to a stop.

Matt shut off the engine. "My ex-wife."

Tasha gazed through the windshield. "So that's her."

"I take it you haven't met her?"

"I only saw her from a distance. She didn't seem to be around much."

Those last few months, his ex had used any excuse to travel.

"She liked France," he said. "She still likes France. There's a man there."

"Oh," Tasha said with obvious understanding.

"Yeah." Matt released his seat belt. "I can't even imagine what she's doing back here."

He and Tasha both stepped out of the car.

"Hello, Dianne," he said as he approached the lit porch.

Her dark hair was pulled back from her face with some kind of headband, the ends of her hair brushing her shoulders. She wore a black wool jacket with leather trim, a pair of black slacks and very high heels. Her makeup was perfect, as always. Her mouth was tight. Her eyes narrowed.

"Where have you been?" she asked. Then her gaze swept Tasha.

"This is Tasha." He didn't like the dismissive expression on Dianne's face. "She and I have been dancing."

He felt Tasha's look of surprise but ignored it.

"What are you doing here?" he asked Dianne.

"I need to speak with you."

Her nostrils flared with an indrawn breath. "It's a private matter."

"Well, I'm not about to end my evening early to listen to you."

Whatever Dianne had to say to him—and he couldn't imagine what that might be—it could wait until morning.

"You can call me tomorrow, Dianne." He started for the door, gesturing for Tasha to go ahead of him.

"It's about François," Dianne blurted out.

Matt kept walking.

Whatever was going on between Dianne and her new

husband was completely their business. Matt couldn't stay far enough away.

"He left me."

Matt paused. "I'm sorry, Dianne. It's none of my business."

"He stole my money."

"Matt?" Tasha said with a little tug against his hand.

"*All* of my money," Dianne said.

"It'll still wait until morning." Matt punched in the key code to his front door. "Do you need me to call you a ride?"

"Matt," Dianne practically wailed.

"We're divorced, Dianne. As I recall, your settlement was more than generous."

Matt had only wanted it to be over. Although his lawyer had argued with him, he'd given her everything she'd asked for. It had meant significant refinancing of the marina, but if he worked hard, he'd be back on solid footing within two or three years.

He retrieved his phone and pulled up his ride app, requesting a car. "Call me tomorrow. I assume you still have my number?"

"I'm in trouble, Matt," Dianne said. "Deep trouble."

"Then I suggest you call a lawyer."

Her voice rose. "I didn't commit a crime."

"I'm glad to hear that. Your car will be here in a couple of minutes."

He opened the door and Tasha went inside.

"How can you be so cruel?" Dianne called out from behind him.

He turned. "How can you have the nerve to ask me to drop everything and deal with your problems? You cheated on me, left me and put my business at risk through your unbridled greed."

A pair of headlights flashed through the trees.

"Your ride is here, Dianne." He stepped through the open door, closing it to then face Tasha.

Matt leaned back against his front door as if he expected his ex-wife to try to break it down.

"Sorry about that," he said.

Tasha wasn't sure how she should feel about the exchange. She knew divorces could be acrimonious, and Matt was within his rights to stay at arm's length from his ex-wife, but Dianne had seemed genuinely upset.

"It sounds like she could use a friend," Tasha said.

"Truthfully, it's hard to know for sure. She's a drama queen. Her reaction to a fire or a flood is the same as her reaction to a broken fingernail."

Tasha tried not to smile. It didn't seem like there was anything funny in the situation.

Matt pushed away from the door. "She was supposed to be in France. She was supposed to stay in France. I'd really hoped she'd stay in France forever. I need a drink. Do you want a drink?"

He started down the short staircase to the glass-walled living room. On the way, he seemed to absently hit a wall switch, and the long fireplace came to life. Fed by gas, it was glassed in on all sides and stretched the length of the living room, separating a kitchen area from a lounge area where white leather armchairs faced a pair of matching sofas.

Tasha knew she should head home. But she found herself curious about Matt, about Dianne, and she'd been sipping on sodas all night long. A real drink sounded appealing.

"I'm thinking tequila," Matt said as he passed one end of the fireplace into the kitchen.

Tasha threw caution to the wind. “I love margaritas.”

“Margaritas it is.” He opened a double-doored stainless steel refrigerator. “We have limes.” He held them up. “Glasses are above the long counter. Pick whatever looks good.”

Feeling happier than she had any right to feel about sharing a drink with Matt, Tasha moved to the opposite end of the kitchen. Near the glass wraparound wall, she opened an upper cupboard, finding a selection of crystal glasses. She chose a pair with deep bowls and sturdy-looking bases.

“Frozen or on the rocks?” he asked.

“Frozen.”

He was cutting limes on an acrylic board. “There should be some coarse salt in the pantry. Through that door.” He pointed with the tip of his knife.

Tasha crossed behind him to the back of the kitchen.

The walk-in pantry was impressive. It was large and lined with shelves of staples and exotic treats.

“Do you like to cook?” she called out to him.

“It’s a hobby.”

She located the coarse salt and reemerged. “I wouldn’t have guessed that.”

“Why?” He seemed puzzled.

“Good question.”

“Thanks.”

“You seem—” she struggled to put it into words “—like the kind of guy who would have a housekeeper.”

“I do.”

“Aha!”

“She’s not a cook. I decided a long time ago that I couldn’t do everything around here and run a business, too, so I chose to do the things I like the best and give up the things I didn’t enjoy.”

"What is it you like best?" Tasha helped herself to one of the limes. She'd spotted some small glass bowls in the cupboard and retrieved one for the salt.

"Cooking, working, the gym."

"Dating?" she asked.

"That's recent."

"But you like it. You do it quite a lot now."

"I do, and I do." He stilled then and seemed to think more about his answer.

"What?" she prompted.

"Nothing. That about sums it up."

"What about friends?"

"Caleb and TJ? Sure. I hang with them whenever I can. With them being so close, we don't really plan anything, we just drop by. It's kind of like background noise."

"Like family," Tasha mused as she cut the lime in half.

She'd observed the relationship between the three men. It was as if they were brothers. She'd like to have close relationships like that. But she had absolutely nothing in common with her two sisters.

"Like family," Matt agreed. "They're going to flip when they find out Dianne's back."

"Do you expect her to stick around?"

It was none of Tasha's business. And she wasn't entitled to have an opinion one way or the other. But she liked that Matt was single. After all, a fantasy was fun only if it had an outside chance of coming true.

The knife slipped, and she cut her finger.

"Ouch!"

"What happened?" He was by her side in an instant.

"I wasn't paying attention."

"Is it bad?" He gently took her hand. "You're bleeding."

"Just a little. Don't let me ruin the drinks."

He seemed amused by her priority as he reached for

a tissue from a box on the counter. "Let's get you a bandage."

"I bet it'll stop on its own." She pressed the tissue against the cut.

"This way." He took her elbow. "We can't have you bleeding into the salt."

He led her up the steps toward the entry hall, but then veered right, taking her down a long hallway with plush silver-gray carpet. Some of the doors were open, and she saw an office and what looked like a comfortable sunroom.

"This is nice," she said.

They entered one room, and it took her only a second to realize it had to be the master bedroom. She hesitated and stumbled.

"Careful," he said.

"This is..."

He paused and glanced around at the king-size bed with taupe accents, two leather and polished metal easy chairs, twin white bedside tables and a polished oak floor with geometric-patterned throw rugs. Here, too, there were walls of windows looking across the bay and over the forest.

"What?" he prompted.

"Big." She settled on the word. She wanted to say *intimidating*, maybe even *arousing*. She was inside Matt's bedroom. How had that happened?

"I know there are bandages in here." He gestured toward the open door to an en suite.

She struggled to even her breathing as she entered the bathroom. "This is big, too."

"I like my space. And I didn't need too many bedrooms, so it was easy to go for something big for the master."

She moved with him to the sink.

"Do you want kids?" She had no idea where that question came from.

He shrugged. "Dianne didn't want them. I'm easy. I could go either way." Then he gave a chuckle as he opened the upper cabinet.

Tasha averted her eyes. Seeing what was in his medicine cabinet seemed far too personal.

"I figure once I meet Caleb's twins," Matt continued, "it'll either make me want some of my own, or cure me of that idea forever."

He set a small bandage on the counter, shut the cabinet and gently removed the tissue from her cut finger.

"I can do this myself," she said, feeling the effects of his closeness.

She liked his smell. She liked his voice. His touch was gentle.

"Two hands are better than one." He turned on the water, waited a moment then tested the temperature.

Tasha could feel her heart tap against her rib cage. Her gaze was caught on his face. He looked inordinately sexy, and amazingly handsome.

"What about you?" he asked, his attention on her finger as he held it under the warm flow of water.

"Huh?" She gave herself a mental shake and shifted her gaze.

"Do you want kids?"

"Sure. I suppose so. Maybe."

"You haven't thought about it?"

She really hadn't. Her focus had been on her career and making it to the top of her profession. "I guess I'm not in any rush."

"Fair enough." He wrapped the small bandage around

the end of her finger and secured it in place. "Good as new."

"Thank you." She made the mistake of looking into his eyes.

His twinkled, and he smiled at her.

For a moment, she thought he was going to kiss her. But instead, he brushed a playful finger across the tip of her nose and stepped back.

"Our ice is melting," he said. "We better blend those drinks."

Sitting across from Dianne at a window table in the Crab Shack, Matt had asked for a water. Now he wished he'd ordered something stronger.

He hadn't wanted to meet her at his house. He was steadily working to move forward with his life; he didn't want to go backward.

"You gave him control of your *entire* portfolio?" Matt couldn't believe what he was hearing.

"He had a mansion," Dianne said, a whine in her tone. "He had a yacht and a jet and memberships at these exclusive clubs. He didn't even want a prenup. Why wouldn't I trust him?"

"Because he was a con artist?"

She gave a pout. "How was I supposed to know that?"

"You weren't," Matt acknowledged. "What you were supposed to do was keep control of your own assets." He was appalled that she would be so blindly trusting of anyone.

"It was all in French," she said. "I couldn't understand it. It only made sense for him to take over the details."

It sounded like the man had taken over a whole lot more than just the details of her assets. He'd obviously taken complete charge of her money. But Matt wasn't about to lengthen the debate. He'd agreed to meet Dianne today, but he had no intention of stepping back into her life, no matter what kind of mess she'd made of it. And by the sounds of it, she'd made a pretty big mess.

Her exotic French husband had taken her money and disappeared, leaving a trail of debts and charges of fraud behind him.

"So, what are you going to do?" he asked her.

She opened her eyes wide, and let her lower lip go soft. "I miss you, Matt."

"Oh, no you don't." He wasn't going there. He so wasn't going there. "What are you going to do, Dianne? *You*, not me. You alone."

Her eyes narrowed, and he stared straight back at her.

Then what looked like fear came over her expression. "I don't know *what* to do."

"Get a job?" he suggested.

The Crab Shack waitress arrived with their lunches, lobster salad for Dianne, a platter of hand-cut halibut and fries for Matt. He had developed a serious fondness for the Crab Shack's signature sauces.

Dianne waited for the waitress to leave. Then she leaned forward, her tone a hiss. "You want me to work? I don't know how to work."

"I don't *want* you to do anything."

"I can't do it, Matt," she said with conviction.

"I'm not going to solve this for you, Dianne." He popped a crispy fry into his mouth.

"You've got loads of money."

"No, I don't. I had to refinance everything to pay your settlement. And even if I did have money, you have no call on it."

"That's my home." She gazed out the window at the cliff side where his house jutted out over the ocean.

"It *was* your home. Temporarily. I paid for the house. Then I paid you half its value in the divorce. Then you sucked out every nickel of my business profits."

"But—"

"Enjoy your lunch, Dianne. Because it's the last thing I'll ever buy for you."

Her mouth worked, but no sounds came out.

"Matt?" Caleb's wife, Jules, arrived to greet him, her tone tentative. She'd obviously caught the expression on his face and Dianne's and knew something was wrong.

He neutralized his own expression. "Jules. How are you?"

Her stomach was well rounded from the twins she was carrying.

"Doing great." She rested a hand on her belly. Then she turned to Dianne, obviously waiting for an introduction.

"Jules, this is my ex-wife, Dianne."

Jules's eyes widened. "Oh."

"She's in town for a short visit."

"I see." It was pretty clear Jules didn't see. As far as Caleb or anybody else knew—including Matt—Dianne had planned to spend the rest of her life in France. "It's nice to meet you, Dianne. Welcome to the Crab Shack."

Dianne didn't respond, her face still tight with obvious anger.

"Are you coming to the chamber of commerce gala?" Matt asked Jules, ignoring Dianne's angry silence.

Jules was coming up on six months pregnant, and her doctor had advised her to keep her feet up as much as possible.

"I'll definitely be there. I'm good for a couple of hours between rests."

"You look fantastic."

Dianne shifted restlessly in her seat, drawing Jules's brief glance.

"You'll be there?" Jules asked Matt.

"I agreed to speak."

"Oh, good. You'll be so much more entertaining than the mayor, and that Neil Himmelsbach they had on Labor Day. I should let you two finish lunch."

Matt rose to give her a quick hug and a kiss on the cheek. "Nice to see you, Jules."

She patted his shoulder. "Better go." Her attention moved to the front entrance, where a customer had just entered the restaurant.

Matt did a double take when he saw it was Tasha. He paused, watching, wondering what she was doing at the Crab Shack.

"Sit *down*," Dianne said to him.

Matt didn't want to sit down. He was waiting to see if Tasha would notice him and react in some way, maybe a wave, maybe a hello, maybe to come over and talk to him.

But she didn't.

"I'll be right back," he said to Dianne, taking matters into his own hands.

"But you—"

He didn't hear the rest.

"Hey, Tasha," he said as he came up to her.

She looked at him in obvious surprise.

"Lunch break?" he asked.

He couldn't help but notice she was dressed in clean jeans and wearing a silky top and her leather jacket. She didn't dress like that for work.

"I started early this morning." It was obviously an explanation for her boss.

"You don't need to punch a time clock with me. Take as long a lunch as you want."

"I'm having lunch with Jules."

"Really?" The revelation surprised Matt. He hadn't realized she and Jules were getting to know each other.

"She invited me," Tasha said.

"That's nice. That's good."

Tasha's gaze strayed past him, and he could tell the moment she spotted Dianne.

"This is going to sound weird," he said, moving in closer and lowering his voice.

"That would be a first."

"Can I kiss you on the cheek? Maybe give you a hug? Just a little one."

Tasha stared up at him. "Are you drunk?"

"No. It's Dianne. It would help me if she thought you and I were… You know…"

"I take it she wants to rekindle something?"

"She wants money above anything else. If she believes I'm with you, it'll stop her from thinking romancing me to get it is an option."

Tasha glanced around the crowded restaurant. It was clear she was checking to see if they knew anyone else here.

"Jules will understand the score," he assured her, assuming she didn't want anyone to get the wrong impression. "I'm sure Caleb's told her all about Dianne."

"I'm not worried about Jules."

"Then what?"

Something was making her hesitate. He dared to hope she was remembering those brief moments in his bathroom when he'd felt a connection to her. Could she be worried about developing feelings for him?

But then her answer was brisk. "Nothing. I'm not worried about anything. Kiss on the cheek. Quick hug. No problem."

Though he was disappointed, Matt smiled his appreciation. “You’re the best.”

“You gave me a twenty percent raise. It’s the least I can do.”

So much for his musings about her feelings for him.

“This is above and beyond,” he whispered as he moved in for the cheek kiss.

She smelled amazing. She tasted fantastic. It was brutal for him to have to pull back.

“You know it is,” she said with a thread of laughter.

He gave her an equally quick hug. “I owe you.”

He squeezed her hands, wishing with all his heart the crowd would disappear from around them and he could be alone with her.

Then he turned away, heading back across the restaurant to where Dianne was glaring at him.

Five

As always, Tasha was impressed with the Crab Shack. During lunch, it was bright and airy, with wooden tables, a casual ambiance and sweeping views of the ocean and cliffs. Then for dinner, they set out white tablecloths, candles and linen, bringing up the outdoor lighting, making it both elegant and cozy. It was no surprise that its popularity was growing fast.

Back in Boston, expensive restaurants had been the norm for her on weekends. She'd been forced to stop whatever it was she was doing far too early in the afternoon, clean up, dress up and go on parade to impress her parents' associates with their three perfect daughters.

She had wasted so much valuable time primping and engaging in inconsequential conversation. To top it off, the food had been absurdly fancy, not at all filling. There were many nights that she'd gone home and made herself a sandwich after dining at a five-star restaurant.

But the Crab Shack wasn't like that. The food was good and the atmosphere comfortable. It was refreshing to be in a place that was high quality without the pretention.

"It's this way," Jules told her, leading a weaving pattern through the tables.

Tasha gave in to temptation and took a final glance at Matt's handsome profile before following.

Jules led her into an office next to the kitchen. "It's a bit crowded in here," she apologized.

"Not a problem."

The square room held a desk with a computer and stacks of papers, a small meeting table with three chairs, and a couple of filing cabinets. It wasn't as bright as the restaurant, but there was a window that faced toward the marina and Caleb's partially built Neo restaurant.

Jules gestured to the table. "I hope you don't mind, I ordered us a bunch of appetizers."

"That sounds great." Tasha wasn't fussy.

"I do better with small things." Jules gave a self-conscious laugh. "That sounds silly. What I mean, is I tend to graze my way through the day rather than attempting a big meal."

"I can imagine your stomach is a bit crowded in there."

Jules was glowing with pregnancy.

"Between the three of us, we do fight for space," Jules said.

Tasha smiled.

Jules opened a laptop on the table. "We have security video files going back three weeks."

"I really appreciate this," Tasha said.

"Caleb has ordered more security cameras, better security cameras with higher resolution. The ones we have now don't show a lot of detail at a distance."

"Anything will help."

Jules moved the mouse and opened the first file.

To say it was boring was an understatement. They set it on a fast speed and sat back to watch.

"Matt's not normally an affectionate guy," Jules mentioned in an overly casual tone.

The observation took Tasha by surprise. It also put her on edge.

"He hugged you," Jules continued, turning her attention from the screen to Tasha. "And he kissed you."

"On the cheek," Tasha said, keeping her own attention on the view of the marina.

The camera angle showed the gate, part of the path and the first thirty feet of the pier. The yachts rocked in fast motion, while people zipped back and forth along the pier and the sun moved toward the horizon.

"It's still odd for him."

"It was for Dianne's benefit," Tasha said. "He wants her to think we're dating."

"They're divorced."

Tasha gave a shrug. "It could be ego, I suppose."

"That doesn't sound like Matt."

Tasha agreed. "Dianne seems to need money. Matt's worried she'll try to latch back onto him."

"Now, *that* sounds like the Dianne I've heard about."

On the video, the lights came up as the sun sank away.

That had been Tasha's impression, as well. "I only met her briefly last night, but—"

"Last night?" The interest in Jules's tone perked up.

"We were coming back from the Edge, and she was waiting for him."

"A date?"

"No." Tasha was careful not to protest too strongly. "A coincidence. I was there talking to the mechanics in the area. I wanted to know if anyone else was having weird engine failures."

"That's a good idea."

"I thought so. Wait, what's that?" Tasha pointed at

the screen. The picture was dark and shadowy, but it looked like someone was scaling the fence. She checked the date and time stamp. "That's the night before *Orca's Run* went out."

"So, it was sabotage."

"Maybe."

They watched the figure move along the pier. It went out of the frame before coming to the slip for *Orca's Run*.

"That has to be it," Jules said.

Tasha wasn't as ready to draw a concrete conclusion. "It didn't look like he was carrying anything, no fuel, no water."

"But he broke in. Whoever it was, was up to no good."

"It's evidence of that," Tasha agreed. She'd hate to assume something and potentially be led in the wrong direction. "We should watch the rest of the video. I can do it myself if you're busy."

"No way. This is the most interesting thing I've done lately. And I'm supposed to sit down every couple of hours." Jules made a show of putting her feet up on the third chair.

There was a light rap on the door, and a waitress pushed it open, arriving with a tray of appetizers and two icy soft drinks.

"I hope you're hungry," Jules said as the server set everything down on the table.

"I'm starving."

"Make sure you try the crab puffs. They're my secret recipe."

"I'm in." Tasha spread a napkin in her lap and helped herself to a crab puff.

"I've been going nuts over smoked salmon," Jules said, going for a decorative morsel on a flat pastry shell. "I don't know why, but my taste buds are big into salt."

Tasha took a bite of the crab puff. It was heavenly. "Mmm," she said around the bite.

Jules's eyes lit up. "See what I mean?"

"You're a genius."

"They're the most popular item on the menu. Caleb wants to steal them for Neo, but I won't let him."

"Stick to your guns," Tasha said before popping the second half of the crab puff into her mouth.

"Oh, I will. We're each half owner of the other's restaurant now, but it's still a competition."

"I hope you're winning. Wait. Take a look." Tasha drew Jules's attention to the laptop screen.

The figure returned to the gate and seemed to toss something over the fence beside it. The two women watched as he climbed the fence, then appeared to look for the object. But then something seemed to startle him, and he ducked away, out of camera range.

"He was up to something," Jules said.

"That was definitely odd," Tasha said. "It could have been tools. I wish we had a better view."

The video got boring again, nothing but yachts bobbing on the midnight tide. Jules took a drink and went for another crab puff.

The office door opened and Caleb appeared.

"How's it going in here?" he asked.

Jules stretched her back as she spoke. "We saw a guy climb over the fence onto the pier and sneak back out again."

Caleb moved past Tasha. He stood behind Jules's chair and began rubbing her shoulders.

"What did he do?" Caleb asked.

"He threw something over the fence," Jules said. "Tasha thinks it might have been tools."

"We couldn't tell for sure," Tasha put in, not wanting to jump to conclusions. "And the frame's not wide enough to see what he did while he was on the pier. It could have been nothing."

The door opened again, and Matt joined them.

"I'll bet it was something," Jules said.

"You'll bet what was something?" Matt asked, glancing around at all three of them.

Tasha couldn't stop herself from reacting to his presence. She imagined his hands on her shoulders, the way Caleb was rubbing Jules's.

"There was a guy," Jules said.

"It might have been something," Tasha jumped in, shaking off the fantasy. "A guy climbing the fence and leaving again. But we couldn't see enough to be sure. There's a lot more video to watch."

"Dianne gone?" Jules asked Matt.

"Hopefully."

"What happened?" Caleb asked. "I didn't expect to see her back in Whiskey Bay…well, ever."

"Neither did I," Matt said. "It turns out her French finance tycoon wasn't all he claimed to be."

"Uh-oh," Caleb said.

"All that money she got in the divorce…"

"No way," Caleb said.

Tasha kept her attention fixed on the screen and away from Matt.

"All gone," he said.

"How is that possible?" Jules asked. "You gave her a fortune."

"The court gave her a fortune," Matt said.

"You didn't fight it."

"I wanted my freedom."

"And she's back anyway," Caleb said. "That didn't work out so well."

"You're not giving her any more money," Jules said.

Tasha wanted to echo the advice, but she didn't feel that it was her business to jump in. Matt and Caleb had been good friends for years. She knew Matt thought of him as a brother.

"I told her to get a job."

"Good advice."

"Let's see if she takes it." Matt didn't sound convinced she would.

Then his hand did come down on Tasha's shoulder. The warmth of his palm surged into her, leaving a tingle behind.

"Anything else going on?"

It was daylight on the video now and people were moving back and forth along the pier: crew, customers, delivery companies and Matt. She watched Matt stride confidently through the frame, and her chest tightened.

She had to struggle to find her voice. "Nothing out of the ordinary. It would be nice to have a wider view."

"You've looked through your own footage?" Caleb asked Matt.

"We have," Matt answered. "But the camera showing the main part of the pier had malfunctioned."

"Malfunctioned?" The skepticism was clear in Caleb's tone.

"We had a technician look at it. The case was cracked. Salt spray got in and caused corrosion. It might be wear and tear, but it could have been pried open on purpose."

"Who would do that?" Caleb asked. "Why would they do that?"

"I wish I knew," Matt said. "I hate to suspect staff, but there are a couple of new hires on the dock. We're checking into their histories."

"Why would staff have to climb the fence?" Caleb asked.

"Not everyone has the combination," Tasha answered. "Not everyone needs it."

"I don't hand it out to the new hires," Matt said.

Tasha knew the footage narrowed the list of suspects—at least of possible staff members as suspects.

"A little to the left," Jules said on a moan.

Caleb smiled down at his wife.

Matt's hand tightened around Tasha's shoulder.

Arousal washed through her with the force of a riptide.

She ordered herself to concentrate. She refocused on the screen, desperately hoping something would happen on the pier to distract her from his touch.

Matt was happy to speak at the chamber of commerce's annual Christmas gala. He knew the chamber did important work. He'd benefited from its programs in the past. Without its loan guarantees, he never could have purchased Whiskey Bay Marina, never mind grown it to the size it was today, or recovered from the financial hit of his divorce for that matter.

He'd started life out in South Boston. There, his father ran a small residential construction company, while his mother did home care for the elderly. His parents had raised six children. Matt was the youngest and easily the most ambitious. His older siblings all still lived in the South Boston area, most working for his father, all raising families of their own.

They seemed content with barbecues and baseball games. But Matt had wanted more. He'd always wanted more out of life. He'd worked construction long enough to put himself through college and set aside a nest egg. Then he'd bought a few fixer-upper houses, sold them for a profit and finally ended up on the West Coast taking what was probably a ridiculous risk on the Whiskey Bay Marina. But it had turned out well.

It seemed people found it an inspiring story.

Finished with his cuff links and his bow tie, he shrugged into his tux jacket. It was custom fitted and made him feel good, confident, like he'd arrived. It was a self-indulgent moment, dressing in an expensive suit for a fine dinner. And he'd admit to enjoying it.

Tonight he had an additional mission. The owners of the three other marinas in the area would be at the gala. A competitor would have a motive for sabotage. Matt had never trusted Stuart Moorlag. He seemed secretive, and Matt had heard stories of him cutting corners on maintenance and overbilling clients. He could have financial troubles.

There was a knock on the front door, and Matt made his way past the living room to the entry hall. He'd ordered a car for the evening to keep from having to drive home after the party.

But it wasn't the driver standing on his porch. It was Tasha.

"We have a problem," she said without preamble, walking into the entry hall.

"Okay."

Then she stopped and looked him up and down. "Wow."

"It's the gala tonight," he said.

"Still. Wow."

"Is *wow* a good thing?"

"You look pretentious."

"So, not good." He told himself he wasn't disappointed. He'd have been surprised if she had liked him in a tux.

He wished she did. But wishing didn't seem to help him when it came to Tasha.

"Good if pretentious was your goal."

"Well, that was a dig."

"I'm sorry. I didn't mean it to sound like that. What I meant was, you'll impress all the people at what I'm guessing is a very fancy event tonight."

"Thanks. I think." It wasn't quite an insult anymore, but it wasn't quite a compliment either. He decided to move on.

He gave a glance to his watch. He had a few minutes, but not long. "What's the problem?"

"The sabotage is escalating."

That got his instant and full attention. Tasha definitely wasn't one to exaggerate.

"How?" he asked.

"I found a peeled wire in the electric system of *Salty Sea*. It seemed suspicious, so I checked further and found a fuel leak."

He didn't understand the significance. "And?"

"Together, they would likely have started a fire."

"Are you *kidding* me?" He couldn't believe what he was hearing.

"I wish I was."

"People could have been *hurt*?"

A fire on a boat was incredibly serious, especially in December. If they had to jump into the water, hypothermia was the likely result.

"Badly," she said.

He didn't want to leave her to attend the gala. He wanted to explore what she'd found, talk this out. He wanted to plan their next move.

"I have to go to the gala," he said, thinking maybe they could meet later. "I'm speaking at it. And the other marina owners will be there. I was going to use it as an excuse to feel them out."

She didn't hesitate. "I want to come."

The statement took him completely by surprise. He couldn't help but take in her outfit of cargo pants, jersey top and a work jacket.

"Not like this," she said, frowning at him.

"Do you have something to wear?"

Her hands went to her hips, shoulders squaring. "You don't think I can clean up, right?"

Registering the determination in her expression—although he had his doubts—he wasn't about to argue that particular point. He looked at his watch again. "I don't have a lot of time. My car will be here in a few minutes."

Her lips pursed in obvious thought. "I don't have a ball gown in my room. But did Dianne leave anything behind? A dress or something?"

"You want to wear my ex-wife's clothes?" Matt was no expert, but that didn't sound like something an ordinary woman would volunteer to do.

"What've you got?"

"You're serious?"

"You don't think I look serious?" she asked.

"You look very serious."

"So?"

He gave up, even though he had major reservations about how this was going to turn out. "There are some things left in the basement. This way." He led her around the corner to the basement stairs.

He flipped the switch as they started down. "She was a shopaholic. Didn't even bother to take all of it with her. Some of the stuff has probably never been worn."

They went past the pool table and entered a cluttered storage room. The dresses were in plastic film, hanging on a rack, jackets and slacks beside them, shoes in boxes beneath. "I hadn't had the time to get rid of it yet."

"I'll be quick," Tasha said, marching up to the rack and searching her way through.

After a few minutes, she chose something red with sparkles.

"Wow," he said.

"You don't think I can pull off red?"

"It's very bold."

"Trust me. I want them to notice." She hunted through the shoe boxes. "I don't suppose you know what size shoe your ex wore?"

"I have no idea."

Tasha held up a black pump, turning it to various angles. Then she straightened, stripped off her boot and fuzzy sock and wiggled her foot into it.

"It'll do," she said.

"Seriously? Just like that?" He'd seen Dianne spend two hours choosing an outfit.

"You said you were in a hurry." Tasha brushed by him.

"Yes, but..."

"Then, let's do this."

He followed behind, shutting off the lights as they went. "You're a strange woman."

"If by *strange*, you mean *efficient*, then thank you."

By *strange*, he meant *unique*. She was like nobody he'd ever met. Not that it was a bad thing. It was a good thing. At the very least, it was an entertaining thing.

"Yes," he said. "I meant efficient."

"Can I borrow your bathroom?"

"Be my guest."

There was another knock on the front door. This time it was sure to be the driver.

"I have to speak at eight," he called to Tasha's back as

she scooted down the hall, clothes bundled in her arms, wearing one work boot and one bare foot.

She waved away his warning, and he turned to answer the door.

Ten minutes later, or maybe it was only five, she emerged from the hallway looking ravishing.

Matt blinked, thinking it had to be an optical illusion. No woman could go from regular Tasha to this screaming ten of a bombshell in five minutes. It wasn't possible.

Her hair was swooped in a wispy updo. The straps of the dress clung to her slim, creamy shoulders. It sparkled with rhinestones as she walked, the full red skirt swishing above her knees. Her green eyes sparkled, the dark lashes framing their beauty. Her lips were deep red, her cheeks flushed, and her limbs were long, toned and graceful.

He couldn't speak.

"Will I do?" she asked, giving him a graceful twirl. Her tone was softer than normal, her words slower and more measured.

He opened his mouth. "Uh…"

"Don't get all fussy on me, Matt. It was a rush job."

"You look terrific."

She glanced down at herself. "Good enough."

"No, not just good enough. Jaw dropping. How did you do that?" How had this gorgeous, feminine creature stayed hidden beneath the baggy clothes and grease all this time?

"I took off my other clothes and put these ones on."

There was more to it than that. "Your hair?"

"Takes about thirty seconds. Are you ready?"

"I'm ready." He was more than ready. He was *so* ready to go on a date with Tasha.

Okay, so they were investigating more than they were dating. And the new information she'd just brought him was unsettling. They'd have to talk more about that in the car.

But she was more ravishingly beautiful than he could have possibly imagined, and she was his partner for the gala. He felt fantastic, far better than he had merely putting on the fine tux, maybe better than he'd felt in his whole life.

At the ballroom in downtown Olympia, Tasha felt like she was stepping into her own past. She'd been to this party dozens of times, the chamber orchestra, the high-end hors d'oeuvres, the glittering women and stiffly dressed men. And, in this case, the rich Christmas decorations, floral arrangements, garlands of holly and evergreen, thousands of white lights, swirls of spun-glass snow and a huge Christmas tree on the back wall, covered in oversize blue and white ornaments and twinkling lights.

"You going to be okay in all this?" Matt asked as they walked through the grand entry.

"I'll be fine." She could do this in her sleep.

"We'll have to sit down near the front. They want me close by for my presentation."

"No problem." She was used to her parents being VIPs at events in Boston. From the time she was seven or eight, she'd learned to sit still through interminable speeches and to respond politely to small talk from her parents' friends and business connections. "Shall we mingle our way down?"

He looked surprised by the suggestion. "Sure."

"Can you point out the other marina owners?"

They began walking as Matt gazed around the room.

"Hello there, Matt." A fiftysomething man approached, clasping Matt's hand in a hearty shake.

"Hugh," Matt responded. "Good to see you again." He immediately turned to Tasha. "This is Tasha Lowell. Tasha, Hugh Mercer owns Mercer Manufacturing, headquartered here in Olympia."

Tasha offered her hand and gave Hugh Mercer a warm smile. "It's a pleasure to meet you, sir." She quickly moved her attention on to the woman standing next to Hugh.

Hugh cleared his throat. "This is my wife, Rebecca."

"Hello, Rebecca," Tasha said, moving close to the woman, half turning away from Hugh and Matt. If she'd learned anything over the years, it was to keep her attention firmly off any man, no matter his age, who had a date by his side. "I *love* that necklace," she said to Rebecca. "A Nischelle?"

Rebecca returned Tasha's smile. "Why, yes. A gift from Hugh for our anniversary."

"How many years?" Tasha asked.

"Twenty-five."

"Congratulations on that. Was it a winter wedding?"

"Spring," Rebecca said. "We were married in New York. My parents lived there at the time."

"I love New York in the spring." Tasha put some enthusiasm in her voice. "Tell me it was a grand affair."

"We held it at Blair Club in the Hamptons."

"Were the cherry blossoms out?" Tasha had been to the Blair Club on a number of occasions. Their gardens were legendary.

"They were."

"It sounds like a dream." Tasha looped her arm through Matt's, taking advantage of a brief lull in the men's conversation. "Darling, I'm really looking forward to some champagne."

He covered her hand. "Of course. Nice to see you, Hugh. Rebecca, you look fantastic."

"Enjoy the party," Hugh said.

Tasha gave a cheery little wave as they moved away.

"*What* was that?" Matt whispered in her ear. "Cherry blossoms? You made it sound like you'd been there."

She didn't want to reveal her past to Matt. She wanted it kept firmly there—in the past.

"Cherry blossoms seemed like a safe bet in the spring. You don't mind my pulling us away from the Mercers, do you? They're not our target."

Too late, it occurred to her that Matt might have some kind of reason for chatting Hugh up. She hoped she hadn't spoiled his plans.

"You were right. They're not our targets." He put a hand on the small of her back. "There. Two o'clock. The man with the burgundy patterned tie."

Ignoring the distraction of Matt's touch, Tasha looked in that direction. "Tall, short brown hair, long nose?"

"Yes. That's Ralph Moretti. He owns Waterside Charters. They're smaller than Whiskey Bay, but they're closest to us geographically."

"Is he married?"

Matt's hand flexed against her waist. "Why?"

"So I know how to play this."

"Play this?"

"If he's up to something, he'll be a lot more likely to give information away based on my giggling, ingenuous questions than if you start grilling him. But if he has a wife who's likely to show up halfway through the conversation, it going to throw us off the game."

"You're going to flirt with him?" Matt did not sound pleased.

"I wouldn't call it flirting."

"What would you call it?"

"Disarming." She sized up Ralph Moretti as they drew closer.

"There's a distinction?" Matt asked.

"Absolutely."

They'd run out of room. Ralph was right there in front of them.

"Moretti," Matt greeted with a handshake.

"Emerson," Ralph responded.

Ralph's guarded tone immediately piqued Tasha's interest.

It took about half a second for his gaze to move to her and stop.

"Tasha Lowell." She offered him her hand.

"Call me Ralph," he told her, lightly shaking. He was gentlemanly enough not to squeeze.

"Ralph," she said with a bright smile. "Matt tells me you have a marina."

"I do indeed."

"I have a thing for boats."

The pressure of Matt's hand increased against her back.

"Really?" Ralph asked, with the barest of gazes at Matt. "What do you like about them?"

"Everything," she said. "The lines of the craft, the motion of the waves, the way they can take you on adventures."

"A woman of good taste," he said.

"How far do you go?" she asked.

Matt coughed.

"Excuse me?" Ralph asked.

Tasha leaned in just a little bit. "Your charters. Oregon? California? Do you go up to Canada?"

"Washington and Oregon mostly," he said.

"Are you looking to expand?"

Ralph's gaze flicked to Matt. Was it a look of guilt?

"Maybe in the future," Ralph said, bringing his attention back to Tasha.

"What about markets?" she asked.

His expression turned confused, maybe slightly suspicious.

"Do you get a lot of women clients?" She breezed past the topic she'd intended to broach. "Party boats. Me and my friends like to have fun."

"Ah," he said, obviously relaxing again. "Yes. Waterside can party it up with the best of them."

"Whiskey Bay—" she touched Matt lightly on the arm "—seems to go for an older crowd."

He stiffened beside her.

She ignored the reaction and carried on. "I don't know if I've seen your advertising. Do you have a website?"

"We're upgrading it," Ralph said.

"Expanding your reach? There is a Midwest full of clients right next door. Spring break would be an awesome time to get their attention."

"Do you have a job?" Ralph asked her.

She laughed. "Are you offering?"

"You'd make one heck of an ambassador."

She held up her palms. "*That's* what I keep telling Matt."

"You're missing the boat on this, Matt." There was an edge of humor to Ralph's tone, but he kept his gaze on Tasha this time.

Matt spoke up. "She can have any job she wants at Whiskey Bay for as long as she wants it."

Ralph quickly glanced up. Whatever he saw on Matt's expression caused him to take a step back.

"It was nice to meet you, Tasha," Ralph said.

"Moretti," Matt said by way of goodbye. Then he steered Tasha away.

"Well, that was interesting," Tasha said.

"Is *that* what you call it?"

"Yes. He wants to expand his business. And something about you put him on edge."

"Because he was trying to steal my date."

"Nah." She didn't buy that. "He reacted when I asked if he was expanding. And he's revamping his website. He's looking to make a move on your customers."

"He's looking to make a move on you."

"Don't be so paranoid."

A wave of mottled mauve silk moved in front of them.

"Hello, Matt."

Tasha was astonished to come face-to-face with Dianne.

"Dianne," Matt said evenly. "What are you doing here?"

"Enjoying the season." She eyed Tasha up and down, a delicate sneer coming over her face as she looked down her nose.

Tasha had seen that expression a thousand times, from women and girls who were certain they were a cut above a plain-looking mechanic and not the least bit hesitant to try to put Tasha in her place.

Still, Tasha felt like she should muster up some sympathy. Dianne was in a tough spot.

"Merry Christmas," she said to Dianne in her most polite voice.

"I see you got out of those oily rags," Dianne returned. "Is that last year's frock?"

"I like to think Bareese is timeless," Tasha said with an air of indifference.

Dianne wrinkled her nose.

Tasha took in Dianne's opulent gown. "Your Moreau must be worth a fortune." She blinked her eyes in mock innocence. "You could auction it after the party. For the funds, I mean."

Matt stifled a laugh.

Dianne's complexion went a shade darker. "Why, you little—"

"Time for us to take our seats," Matt said, taking Tasha's hand. "What is up with you?" he asked as they moved away.

Tasha winced. "I'm sorry. I shouldn't have said that."

"That's not what I meant."

"It was really rude."

The lights blinked, and the MC made his way onto the stage.

"Dianne was the one who was rude. And I'm grateful," Matt continued, picking up the pace. "You keep it up, and she's going to leave town in a hurry. Besides, she deserves a little of her own medicine for once."

Matt's odd compliment warmed Tasha. She wasn't particularly proud of going mean-girl debutante on Dianne. But Matt's life would be better if Dianne left. And Tasha found she wanted that, too.

Six

Matt's speech had gone well. People had laughed in the right spots and clapped in the right spots. He was happy to have been entertaining. But he was happier still to watch Tasha's face in the front row. Every time she'd smiled, he'd felt a physical jolt.

He couldn't believe how feminine, how beautiful, how downright elegant she'd looked surrounded by the splendor of the ballroom. And now, swaying in his arms, she was graceful and light. The transformation was astonishing. Cinderella had nothing on Tasha.

"You've done this before," he guessed as he guided her into a slow spin.

"Danced? Yes, I have."

"Been the belle of a ball."

She smiled at that as she came back into his arms. "I'm far from the belle of any ball."

The dance floor was nicely filled. The music was superb, and beautiful women floated past on the arms of their partners. None could hold a candle to Tasha.

"You are to me," he said.

"You're flirting?"

"No. I'm disarming."

She gave a short laugh. "It's not going to work."

He supposed not. "You have definitely done this before."

"I've been to a few balls in my time."

"I never would have guessed. I mean before tonight I never would have guessed. You sure don't let on that there's an elegant lifestyle in your past."

"I don't spend much time dwelling on it."

"You're very good at this." He'd been stunned at her ability to make small talk, to get the other marina owners to relax and be chatty. They hadn't come up with any solid leads or suspects, but they'd learned Waterside Charters was expanding and Rose and Company was taking delivery of a new seventy-five-foot yacht in the spring. Both would be competing head-to-head with Whiskey Bay Marina.

"You don't have to like something to be good at it."

"Do you like dancing?" he asked, wanting to hear that she did, hoping to hear that she liked dancing with him.

"Yes. But not necessarily in these shoes."

He glanced down. "Do they hurt?"

"You've never worn high heels before, have you?"

"That would be a no."

"Yes, they hurt. They don't fit all that well."

"Should we stop?"

"I'll survive."

He debated finding them a place to sit down. But he liked having her in his arms. So he settled for slowing the pace, inching even closer to her. It was a good decision.

"So where did you attend these formative balls?"

"Boston, mostly. Some in New York. Once in DC when I was around seventeen."

"You're a fellow Bostonian?" He was surprised by the idea.

She drew back to look at him. "You, too?"

"Southie."

"And you left?" She seemed to be the one surprised now.

"I did. The rest of my family stayed in the neighborhood, though."

The song ended, and another started. He danced them right through the change.

"Brothers and sisters?" she asked.

"Three brothers, two sisters. I'm the youngest. What about you?"

"Wow. Six kids?"

"Yep."

"Your parents must have been busy."

"It was busy and crowded. I had absolutely no desire to live like that. Where did you grow up?"

Since she'd talked about balls and flying off to New York and Washington for parties, he was guessing she wasn't a Southie.

It took her a minute to answer. "Beacon Hill."

So, she had lived posh.

"It's nice up there," he said.

"It's snooty up there. At least the people I knew, and especially my parents' friends and associates. I couldn't wait to get away from their judgment."

"Spread your wings?" he asked.

"Something like that. Yes, very much like that."

He found the insight quite fascinating. "Does your family still live there?" For some reason, learning she was from Boston made their connection seem stronger.

"Absolutely."

"Brothers and sisters?" he asked when she didn't offer details.

"Two sisters. Youngest here, too," she said with an almost guilty smile.

"Makes it easy to get away with things," he said.

"Made it easy to slip town."

"Are you close to them?"

He'd never heard her talk about her family. Then again, they hadn't had a whole lot of in-depth conversations about either of their backgrounds. Mostly he liked to leave his alone.

"We don't have a lot in common." There was something in her tone, not regret exactly, but acceptance of some kind.

"I hear you," he said, recognizing the emotion.

He and his family seemed to operate in different dimensions. He saw value in financial success. He'd worked hard to get here, and he had no problem enjoying it. The rest of his family held financial success in suspicion. He'd tried to get his mind around it, but at the end of the day he just couldn't agree.

Dianne had understood. It was one of the things that first drew him to her. She liked the finer things, and was unapologetic about her ambition. That trait might have turned on her now. But the theory was still sound. He was still going after success.

"My family..." he began, wondering how to frame it. "They're content to pay the bills, throw potlucks on Sundays, take their kids to community center dance lessons and cheer for the Red Sox at tailgate parties."

"Oh, the horror," she mocked.

"I want more," he said.

"Why?"

"Why not?" He looked around the ballroom. "This is

nice. This is great. And who wouldn't want the freedom to take any trip, eat at any restaurant, accept any party invitation."

"Are you free, Matt? Really?"

"I'm pretty damn free."

His choice of lifestyle had allowed him to work hard, to focus on his business, to succeed in a way that was satisfying to him. If he'd strapped on a tool belt in Southie, met a nice woman and had a few kids, it would have meant being dishonest about himself.

It was Tasha's turn to look around the room. "This all doesn't feel like a straitjacket to you?"

"Not at all." He didn't understand her attitude. She seemed to be having a good time. "And I'm here by choice."

"These people don't seem disingenuous to you?"

"Maybe the ones that are sabotaging my boats. But we're not even sure they're here. It's just as likely they're at the Edge."

"What's wrong with the Edge?"

"Nothing. Did I say there was something wrong with the Edge?"

"You used it as a negative comparator to this party."

"It's a whole lot different than this party. Like Beacon Hill and Southie. Do you honestly think people prefer Southie?"

"They might."

Matt wasn't buying the argument. "Sure. People from Southie are proud. I get that. Believe me, I've lived that. But you give them a real and serious choice, they'd be in Beacon Hill in a heartbeat."

Tasha's steps slowed. "It's kind of sad that you believe that."

"It's not sad. And I don't just believe that. It's true."

She stopped. "Thanks for the dance, Matt."

"You can't honestly be annoyed with me." It wasn't reasonable.

"I'm going to rest my feet."

"I'll take you—"

"No." She put her hand on his chest and moved back. "Go mingle. I'll see you later on."

"Tasha." He couldn't believe she was walking away.

Tasha wasn't angry with Matt. She felt more sad than anything.

Sure, he'd made some money in his life. But up to now he'd struck her as being mostly down-to-earth. She'd thought the money was incidental to him, running a business that he loved. It was disappointing to discover that his goal had been wealth.

Seeing him tonight, she realized her initial instincts were right. He was exactly the kind of man she'd left behind. Ironically, he was the kind of man her parents would love.

If this were a Boston party, her parents would be throwing her into his arms. The Lowells were an old Bostonian family, but her parents wouldn't hold Matt's Southie roots against him, not like her grandparents or great-grandparents would have.

In this day and age, money was money. Her father in particular respected men who pulled themselves up from nothing. It was a darn good thing they weren't back in Boston right now.

She crossed the relative quiet of the foyer, following the signs to the ladies' room. She needed to freshen up. Then she really was going to find a place to sit down and rest her feet. The shoes might be slightly large, but they were also slightly narrow for her feet, and she had developed stinging blisters on both of her baby toes.

As she passed an alcove, she caught sight of Dianne's unmistakable mauve dress. Dianne was sitting on a small bench, gazing out a bay window at the city lights. Her shoulders were hunched, and they were shaking.

Tasha felt like a heel. One of the reasons she avoided these upper-crust events was that they brought out the worst in her. She seemed too easily influenced by the snobbery and spitefulness.

The last thing in the world she wanted to do was comfort Matt's ex-wife. But it was partly her fault that Dianne was upset. She'd been insufferably rude in suggesting she auction off her dress.

Tasha took a turn and crossed the alcove, coming up beside Dianne.

Dianne looked up in what appeared to be horror. She quickly swiped her hand beneath her eyes. But the action did nothing to hide the red puffiness.

"Are you okay?" Tasha asked.

"I'm fine." Dianne gave a jerky nod. "Fine."

It was patently obvious it was a lie.

Tasha gave an inward sigh and sat down on the other end of the padded French provincial bench. "You don't look fine."

"I got something in my eyes. Or maybe it was the perfume. Allergies, you know."

Tasha told herself to accept the explanation and walk away. She didn't know Dianne. Given the circumstances, fake though her relationship with Matt was, she was likely the last person Dianne wanted to talk to. But it would be heartless to simply leave her there.

"You're obviously upset," Tasha said.

"Aren't *you* the observant one."

"Don't."

"Why? What do you want? To rub my nose in it? Again?"

"No. I want to apologize. I was nasty to you earlier. I'm really sorry about that. I thought you were…" Tasha struggled for the right words. "Stronger. I thought you were tough. I didn't mean to upset you."

Dianne's tone changed. "It's not you. It's…" She closed her eyes for a long second. A couple of more tears leaked out. "I can't," she said.

Tasha moved closer. She put a hand on Dianne's arm. "Will talking to me make it any worse?"

Dianne drew in a shuddering breath. She opened her eyes and gazed at Tasha for a long time.

"I've made such a mess of it," she finally said.

"You mean losing the money?"

Dianne nodded. "François was charming, attentive, affectionate. Matt was working all the time. He never wanted to travel with me. I thought… I thought our life together would be different. But it wasn't any fun. It was all work, work, work. And then I met François. It wasn't on purpose. I'm not a bad person."

"I don't think you're a bad person." Tasha was being honest about that.

Dianne might not be the right person for Matt, and maybe she had a selfish streak, but right now she just seemed sad and defeated. Tasha would have to be made of stone not to feel sympathy.

Dianne gave a brittle laugh. "I thought François not wanting a prenup was the perfect sign, the proof that he loved me for me. He seemed to have so much more money than I did. And he'd invested so successfully, that I thought I couldn't lose…but I did lose. And I'd hoped Matt…"

"What exactly do you want from Matt?" Tasha might be sympathetic, but she knew sympathy alone wouldn't help Dianne.

Dianne shrugged. "At first… At first I thought there might still be a chance for us. I was the one who left him, not the other way around. I thought he might still…" She shook her head. "But then I met you, and I realized he'd moved on."

A part of Tasha wanted to confess. But she knew Matt wouldn't consider a reconciliation with Dianne. And telling Dianne she and Matt weren't dating would be a betrayal of him. She couldn't do it.

"So, now what?" Tasha asked.

"I don't know." Dianne's tears welled up again. "I honestly don't know."

"You need to know," Tasha said as gently as she could. "You need a plan. You need to take care of yourself."

"I can't."

"You can. Everyone can. It's a matter of finding your strengths."

"My strength is marrying rich men."

"That's not true. It's not your only strength. And even if it was your only strength, it's a bad strength, not one you want to depend on. Look what happened last time."

"I have no money," Dianne said, looking truly terrified. "I've nearly maxed out my credit cards. I've missed payments. They're going to cancel them. I really will be selling my clothes on the street corner."

"Okay, now you're being melodramatic."

"I'm not," she moaned.

"What about your family? Could you stay with family?"

Dianne gave a choppy shake of her head. "There's no one."

"No one at all?"

"My dad died. My stepmother sent me to boarding school. She couldn't wait to get me out of the house."

"Are they in Washington State?"

"Boston."

Tasha was surprised. "You, too?"

Dianne stilled. "You're from Boston?"

"I am."

Dianne searched Tasha's face. "You're a Lowell. *The* Lowells?"

Tasha was embarrassed. "I don't know if there are any 'the' Lowells."

"The Vincent Lowell Library?"

"My grandfather," Tasha admitted.

"Does Matt know?" Before Tasha could respond, Dianne continued on a slightly shrill laugh. "Of course he knows. Why didn't I see that before? You're his dream match."

Tasha was confident Matt didn't know. And there wasn't much to know anyway. The Lowells might be an old Boston family. But there were plenty of those around. It wasn't all that noteworthy.

"Do you want to go back to Boston?" Tasha asked, turning the subject back to Dianne.

"No. Never. That's not in the cards."

"Do you want to stay here?" Tasha was trying to find a starting point, any starting point for Dianne.

Dianne lifted her head and looked around. "There's nothing left for me here either." Her voice cracked again. "Not without Matt."

"You really need to think about a job. You're young. Get started on a career. Did you go to college?"

"Only for a year. I took fine arts. I didn't pass much."

"What would you like to do? What are you good at?"

Dianne looked Tasha in the eyes. “Why are you doing this?”

“I want to help,” Tasha answered honestly.

“Why? I’m nothing to you.”

“You’re a fellow human being, a fellow Bostonian, part of the sisterhood.”

Dianne gave a hollow laugh. “There’s no sisterhood. Are you a do-gooder? Am I a charitable thing for you?”

“No.” Tasha gave it some thought. “I don’t know, really.” It was as honest as she could be.

“I gave parties,” Dianne said in a tired, self-mocking voice. “I can make small talk and order hors d’oeuvres.”

The germ of an idea came to Tasha.

Caleb had fancy restaurants all over the country. Perhaps Jules, Tasha knew her better than she did Caleb, might be willing to help Dianne.

“I’m going to ask around,” Tasha said.

“Matt won’t like that.”

“Doesn’t matter.” Tasha wasn’t sure if Matt would care or not. But surely he’d be in favor of anything that put Dianne back on her feet, helped her to take care of herself.

She didn’t have to make a big deal with Jules. And if Matt did find out, he’d see the logic and reason, she assured herself. He was a very reasonable man.

On the drive home, Tasha seemed lost in thought. Either that, or she was still annoyed with Matt for appreciating financial security. He’d wanted to talk about it some more, maybe help her understand his motivations. But he didn’t want to rekindle their argument. He liked it better when they were on the same side of something.

“Could we really have had a fire?” he asked her.

She turned from where she’d been gazing out the window into the darkness. “What?”

"On *Salty Sea*. Would there have been a fire?"

"Yes. Almost certainly. The fuel from the fuel line leak would have sprayed across the spark from the electric short, and *bam*, it would have ignited."

"It looks odd," he said. "You talking about the inner workings of an engine while you're dressed like that."

"That's why I don't dress like this."

"You look terrific."

"I feel like a fraud. I can't wait to get out of this getup." She reached down and peeled off the black pumps.

The action was sexy, very sexy. He immediately imagined her shrugging down the straps of the dress. He shifted in his seat.

"Feet sore?" he asked.

"And how. Steel-toed boots might be clunky, but they're built for wearing, not for show."

"They wouldn't go with the dress."

"Ha ha."

"And it would be hard to dance in them."

Tasha curled her legs up on the seat, a hand going to one foot to rub it. "I'd be willing to give it a shot."

Matt curled his hands to keep them still. "The new cameras are being installed tomorrow."

"We need them. I'm doubling up on my inspections. Alex and I are going to check every boat the morning before it leaves port."

"Won't that be a lot of work?"

"I couldn't do everything I'd like, not without hiring three more mechanics. But we can cover the basics."

"Do you need to hire someone else?"

She switched her self-massage to the other foot. "I'll call in all the contract mechanics. But I have to believe this is temporary. The next time that guy tries something, we're going to catch him on camera and have him arrested."

Matt gave in to temptation and reached across the back seat for one of her feet.

"Don't." She jumped at his touch.

He looked meaningfully at the driver. "It's just a foot."

"That's not a good idea."

He ignored her, settling her foot in his lap and pressing his thumb into the arch.

She gave a small moan.

"Those blisters look awful," he said.

Her baby toes and the backs of her heels were swollen and red.

"They'll heal."

"Why didn't you say something?"

"I did."

"You didn't tell me how bad it was." He massaged carefully around the swollen skin.

"That feels good," she said.

"Do you need to take the day off tomorrow?"

"You're funny."

"I'm serious. It's Sunday. Don't work."

"And let Alex do it all?"

He didn't have a comeback for that. He had to admire Tasha's work ethic. Still, he couldn't let her burn herself out. And her feet were going to be painful tomorrow.

"As long as I don't put on the same shoes," she said. "I'll use bandages and wear thick socks. I'll be fine."

"You're a trouper," he said with honest admiration.

The driver slowed as Matt's driveway came up on the right.

"You're easily impressed," she said.

"Not really."

They were silent as the car cruised through the trees to

the house. While they did, Matt continued his massage. His image of her strong and sturdy on the job faded to how she was now…soft, smooth, almost delicate.

When the car came to a stop, he reached to the floor and collected her shoes.

"What are you doing?" she asked.

"Wait right there." He exited from his side and tipped the driver.

Then he went around to her, opening the door and reaching in to lift her from the seat.

"Oh, no you don't," she protested.

"Oh, yes I do. You can't put these shoes back on. You'll burst the blisters and bleed all over the place."

"Then I'll walk barefoot."

"Over the rocks and through the mud? Hang on."

"Put me down."

But even as she protested, he hoisted her easily into the air, and her arms went around his shoulders. He pushed the sedan door shut with his shoulder and started to the stairs that led to the staff quarters.

"This is ridiculous," she said. "Nobody better see us."

"It's dark."

"There are lights on the porch."

"It's after midnight. Everyone will be asleep."

"They better be."

He couldn't help but smile to himself. He'd learned by now that Tasha hated anything that made her look remotely weak.

"Blisters are nothing to be ashamed of," he said.

"I'm not ashamed of having blisters." She paused. "I'm ashamed of having some Neanderthal carry my apparently feeble self to my room."

"I'm wearing a tux."

"So?"

"I'm just saying, your average Neanderthal probably didn't wear a tux."

The joke got him a bop in the shoulder.

"Not much of a comeback," he said.

"We're here. You can put me down now."

"Not yet." He mounted the stairs for the second floor.

She squirmed in his arms. "I can walk on wooden stairs in my bare feet."

"Splinters."

"I'm not going to get splinters."

"We're here. Where's your key?"

"You can put me down on the mat."

"I like holding you." He did. He was in absolutely no hurry to put her down. "You're light. You're soft. Your hair smells like vanilla."

"It's not locked," she said.

"Are you kidding me?" he barked. "With all that's been going on?" He couldn't believe she would be so cavalier about her own safety.

He reached for the doorknob and opened the door. He set her down on the floor inside and immediately turned on the light switch, checking all the corners of the room, the small sitting area, the kitchenette, the double bed. Then he crossed to the bathroom and opened up the door.

"Matt, this is silly."

He was annoyed with her. No, he was downright angry. Somebody was targeting them for unknown reasons, and so far it had more to do with her than with anybody else at Whiskey Bay, and she was leaving her door unlocked?

He turned back. "Please tell me you lock it at night."

She looked decidedly guilty. "I can start."

He took the paces that brought him in front of her.

"You bet your life you're going to start. You're going to start tonight, now, right away."

"You don't need to get upset," she said.

"You're scaring me." His gaze fell on her gorgeous green eyes. "I'm afraid for you." He took in her flushed cheeks. "I want to protect you. I…"

Their gazes meshed, and the sound of the surf filled the silence. She just stood there in the shadows looking like his fondest dream come true.

She looked delicate and enticing. Her hair was mussed. One strap had fallen down, leaving her shoulder bare. He wanted to kiss her shoulder. He wanted to taste that shoulder more than he'd ever wanted anything in his life.

He gave in.

He leaned forward, gently wrapping his hands around her upper arms. He placed a light kiss on her shoulder. Then he tasted her skin with the tip of his tongue. He kissed her again, made his way to her neck.

She tipped her head sideways, giving him better access.

He brushed her hair back, kissing his way to her ear, her temple, her closed eyes and finally her mouth.

She kissed him back, and he spread his fingers into her hair.

She stepped into his arms, an enchanting, elegant, utterly feminine woman pressing against his hard, heated body.

He reached out and pushed the door shut behind her.

He deepened their kiss.

He began to unzip her dress, paused, running his hands over the smooth skin of her back.

"Don't stop," she gasped. "Don't, don't stop."

Seven

Everything flooded from Tasha's mind, everything except the taste of Matt's lips, the feel of his hands and the sound of his voice. His heart beat against her chest where they pressed together. She wanted this. No, she needed this. Whatever it was that had been building between them for days on end was bursting out, and there was no stopping it.

She pushed off his tux jacket, and he tossed it on the chair. She tugged his bow tie loose, and it dangled around his neck. She kissed his square chin, struggled with the buttons of his shirt, while his hands roamed her back.

His hands were warm, the fingertips calloused. As she peeled away his tuxedo, the urbane facade seemed to melt away along with it. He was tough underneath, muscular and masculine. A small scar marred his chest, another across his shoulder.

She kissed the shoulder and traced a fingertip along his chest. "What happened?"

"Working," he answered, his breathing deep. "Winch handle and a rogue wave."

"You should be more careful."

"I will."

She couldn't help but smile at his easy capitulation.

His hands went to her dress straps. He eased them down, baring her breasts in the cool air.

"Gorgeous," he said stopping to stare.

It had been a long time since a man had seen her naked, never if you didn't count an eighteen-year-old freshman. She was glad it was Matt, glad he seemed pleased, happy to bask in the heat of his gaze.

He slowly reached out, brushing his thumb across her nipple. She sucked in a breath, a shudder running through to her core. She closed her eyes, waiting for him to do it again.

"Oh, Tasha," he whispered, his hand closing over her breasts.

She tipped her head for his kiss, and her dress slithered to the floor.

His palms slipped to her rear, covering her satin panties. His lips found hers again, his kiss deep and delicious. His shirt separated, and they were skin to skin.

"You're so soft." His hand continued its exploration of her breast.

Rockets of sensation streamed from her hard nipples to the apex of her thighs.

Impatient, she reached for his belt, looping it free, popping the button of his pants and dragging down the zipper.

He groaned as her knuckles grazed him.

Then he scooped her back into his arms and carried her to the double bed, stripping back the blankets to lay her on the cool sheets. He was beside her in a moment, shucking his pants.

He came to his knees, hooking his thumbs in the waist

of her panties, drawing them slowly down, to her thighs, to her knees and over her ankles.

He kissed her ankle, then her knee, then her thigh and her hip bone, making his way to her breasts, kissing them both, making her heartbeat echo all through her.

She raked her fingers into his hair. A buzzing started within her, making her twitch with need.

"You have a condom?" she asked breathlessly. She was woefully unprepared.

"I've got it," he said. "Don't worry."

He rose up and kissed her mouth. Then his hands went on a glorious exploration, touching her everywhere, discovering secrets, making her writhe with impatience and need.

"Please, Matt," she finally whimpered.

"Oh, yes," he said, levering above her, stroking her thighs. She watched him closely as he pressed slowly, steadily inside.

She rocked her hips upward, closing her legs around him.

He moved, pulling out, pushing in, grasping her to him as he kissed her deeper and deeper. She met his tongue thrust for thrust, and her hands gripped his back. She needed an anchor as gravity gave way.

The room grew hotter. The waves sounded louder on the rocks below. Matt's body moved faster, and she arched to meet him, the rhythm increasing.

Fulfillment started as a deep glow, burning hotter, moving outward, taking over her belly, then her breasts, then her legs and her arms. It tingled in her toes and in the roots of her hair. She cried out as sensation lifted her. Then she flew and then floated.

"Tasha," Matt cried, his body shuddering against her.

She absorbed every tremor, his body slick, his heartbeat steady. Her waves of pleasure were unending, until she finally fell still, exhausted, unable to move beneath his comfortable weight on top of her.

She didn't know what she'd done.

Okay, she knew what she'd done. She knew exactly what she'd done. She also knew she shouldn't have done it.

"Stop," he muttered in her ear.

"Stop what?"

He rose up on an elbow. "I can feel you second-guessing yourself."

"We can't undo that," she said.

"Who wants to undo it?"

"We do. We should. That wasn't part of the plan."

"There was a plan?"

"Quit laughing at me."

He enveloped her in a warm hug.

It shouldn't have felt so great. It couldn't feel this great.

"Oh, Tasha. We made love. People do it all the time. The world will keep spinning, I promise."

"Maybe *you* do it all the time."

"I didn't mean that the way it sounded." He eased back to look at her again. He smoothed the hair from her eyes. "I don't do it all the time. My marriage was on the rocks for quite a while. And since then… Well, I've only just started dating again."

Tasha shouldn't have cared whom Matt had been with before her. But she found herself glad that he hadn't had an active sex life. She didn't want it to matter, but it did.

"I'm—" She stopped short, realizing she was going to sound hopelessly unsophisticated.

His eyes widened, and he drew sharply back. "You weren't…"

"A virgin? No. I would have said something."

"Thank goodness."

"I did have a boyfriend," she said. "Right after high school."

"One?" Matt asked. "Singular?"

"I couldn't date anyone in trade school. There were three women in a class of thirty-six. We were way too smart to get involved with anyone. It could have killed our chances of being treated as peers."

"I suppose," Matt said. Then he touched a finger to the bottom of her chin. "So, you're saying one then? Just the one guy?"

"Just the one," she admitted, feeling a bit foolish. She should have kept her mouth shut.

"Tasha Lowell." His kissed her tenderly on the mouth. "I am honored."

"Oh, that didn't sound outmoded at all."

He grinned. "You could be honored back at me."

"Okay," she said, fighting a smile. "Matt Emerson, I am honored. And I'm embarrassed. And I'm certainly soon to be regretful."

"But not yet?" he asked on an exaggerated note of hopefulness.

"I can feel it coming."

"You have nothing to regret."

She wriggled to relieve the pressure on her hip, and he eased off to one side.

"You said that about our kiss," she said, sitting up and pulling a sheet over her breasts.

"Did you?" He traced a line along her knuckles.

"I don't know." Things had changed so fundamentally between them. Was that single kiss to blame?

She didn't want to talk about it right now. She didn't want to dissect this.

"I could stay," he offered in a soft voice.

She jumped an inch off the bed and her voice rose an octave. "What?"

"I don't have to rush off."

"Yes, you do." She looked around for her clothes, realizing she needed to get out of the bed right now. "You can't stay here. It's the staff quarters. You need to get out while it's still dark, before anybody starts work."

He didn't look happy. But he also seemed to understand. "I know. This isn't exactly discreet. But I don't want to leave you." He reached for her.

She evaded his grasp. "If you don't. If somebody sees you, then it's trade school all over again. Only this time I had a one-night stand with the teacher."

His brow went up. "How am I the teacher?"

"You know what I mean. You're in a position of authority. It's worse than sleeping with a peer. I lose any and all credibility. Everybody's reminded that I'm not one of the guys."

"They respect you, Tasha. And who says this is a one-night stand?"

"Who says it's not? So far that's exactly what it is."

"But—"

"But nothing, Matt. The mathematical odds that this leads to something, I mean something besides a fling based on chemistry alone, are, I don't know, maybe five, six percent. The mathematical odds of this leading to the dismantling of my credibility and reputation are around ninety. What would you do if you were me?"

"Where did you come up with five or six percent?"

"I did a quick calculation in my head."

"That's insane." He reached for her again, and she backed to an ever safer distance.

She didn't want him to leave. But he had to leave. He had to leave now before she weakened.

"Please, Matt," she said.

He hardened his jaw. "Of course." He threw back the covers and came to his feet.

She didn't want to watch him walk naked across the room. But she couldn't help herself. He was magnificent, and the sight of him brought back instant memories of their lovemaking.

Her skin flushed. Then goose bumps formed. But she had to be strong. She would force herself to let him leave.

With Noah Glover's electric expertise to guide them, Matt, Caleb and TJ had spent the day installing the new security cameras. Now as a thank-you, Matt was hosting dinner for Caleb and Jules, TJ and Jules's sister, Melissa, along with Noah.

Watching Caleb with Jules, and Noah with Melissa, Matt couldn't help thinking about Tasha. She'd made herself scarce all day, while he'd spent most of it watching for her. He couldn't stop thinking about her. He'd lain awake half the night thinking about her, wishing he could have slept with her. After their mind-blowing lovemaking, his arms felt completely empty without her.

"I hope the extra cameras do the trick," TJ said as he joined Matt by the dining table.

Matt was setting out plates and glasses, since Jules had all but kicked him out of the kitchen.

"I don't care what it takes," Matt responded. "I'm catching this guy and throwing him in jail. His last stunt could have caused a fire. People could have been seriously hurt, or worse."

"Your competition?" TJ asked, gazing through the glass wall to the marina below.

"I talked to all of them at the gala last night. Waterside Charters is expanding, and Rose and Company bought a new seventy-five-footer. Both would be happy to steal business from me. But I don't see them doing it this way."

"Then what?" TJ asked.

"If I have my way, we'll find out soon." Matt took in the overview of the marina, his gaze settling on the staff quarters. Tasha was there.

Giving up fighting with himself, he extracted his cell phone. "I'll just be a minute," he said to TJ, then moved down the hall.

He typed into his phone: Dinner with Caleb and Jules at my place. Talking about the new cameras. Can you come?

He hit Send and waited. It was a stretch of an excuse, but he didn't care. He wanted her here with him.

Jules and Melissa were laughing in the kitchen. TJ's voice blended with Caleb's and Noah's. Everybody sounded happy. It had been a good day's work. It was a good night with friends. Matt should have felt terrific.

His phone pinged with Tasha's response. Just leaving. Meeting some people for drinks.

Disappointment thudded hard in his stomach. He wanted to ask who. He wanted to ask where. Mostly, he wanted to ask why she'd choose them over him.

"Hey, Matt?" Noah appeared and moved down the hall toward him.

"Hi. Thanks again for your help today."

"Sure." Noah looked nervous.

"What's up?" Matt asked.

Noah glanced down the hall behind him. "You mind if I hijack dessert tonight?"

"You brought dessert?"

"No, no. I brought a bottle of champagne."

Matt waited for the explanation.

"And this," Noah said, producing a small velvet box.

There was no mistaking the shape of the box.

"Are you serious?" Matt asked, surprised.

Noah flipped it open to reveal a diamond solitaire. "Dead serious."

"Are you sure?" Matt lowered his voice. "I mean, not are you sure you want to propose, Melissa is amazing. Are you sure you want to do it in front of us?"

Noah gave a self-conscious grin. "You've all been fantastic. You're all family. I really think she'd want to share the moment."

"That's a bold move. But you know her better than the rest of us. Well, maybe not better than Jules. Does Jules know?"

"Nobody knows."

"Okay." Matt couldn't help but grin. He had to admire Noah for this one. "Dessert's all yours."

Noah snapped the ring box shut and tucked it back in his pocket.

Matt slapped him on the shoulder as they turned for the living room. "I thought you looked a little overdressed tonight."

It was rare for Noah to wear a pressed shirt, jacket and slacks. He was more a blue jeans kind of guy.

"Everything's ready," Jules called out from the kitchen.

"Let's get this show on the road," Melissa added.

Matt and TJ took the ends of the rectangular table, with Caleb and Jules along the glass wall, and Noah and Melissa facing the view.

Matt lit the candles and Caleb poured the wine. Caleb had the best-stocked cellar, and he always brought along a few bottles. Matt had long since given up trying to compete.

"Why haven't you decorated for the holidays?" Jules

asked Matt, gazing around the room. "No tinsel? No tree?"

Caleb gave a grin as he held the baked salmon platter for Jules. "Our place looks like Rockefeller Square attacked the North Pole."

"You don't even have a string of lights," Melissa said, helping herself to a roll.

"There's not a lot of point." Matt wasn't about to put up the decorations he'd shared with Dianne. And he didn't care enough to go shopping for more.

"Is it depressing?" Jules asked him, looking worried. "Being here on your own for Christmas?"

Depressed was the last thing Matt was feeling. Relieved was more like it. The last Christmas with Dianne had been painful.

"I'm fine," he told Jules. "I'm just not feeling it this year."

"Well, I can't stand it," Melissa said. "We need to do something. You do have decorations, right?"

"Whoa," Noah said. "That's up to Matt."

"No big deal," Matt was quick to put in. The last thing he wanted was for Noah and Melissa to get into an argument tonight.

"He needs new stuff," TJ said. "That's what I did. Well, I waited one Christmas." He sobered as he added some salad to his plate.

The table went silent, remembering the loss of TJ's wife.

He looked up at the quiet table. "Oh, no you don't. It's been two years. I'm all right, and I'm looking forward to Christmas this year."

"You'll come to our place," Jules said. "You'll *all* come to our place."

"We can figure it out closer to the day." Matt didn't want to hold her to the impulsive invitation.

It was her first Christmas with Caleb. And Noah and Melissa would be engaged. The two sisters were working through a rocky, although improving, relationship with their father. They might not need a big crowd around them.

Matt's thoughts went back to Tasha. He wondered to what she'd done last year for Christmas. Had she gone home for a few days? Had she celebrated here with friends? He didn't know. He was definitely going to ask.

Conversation went on, and it was easy for him to coast. He laughed in the right places, made the odd comment, but his mind wasn't there. It was with Tasha, where she'd gone, what she was doing, whom she was doing it with.

As they finished eating, Matt cleared away the plates while Jules cut into the chocolate hazelnut layer cake. He couldn't take any credit for it. A local bakery, Persichetti, had delivered it earlier in the day.

"I love Persichetti cake," Melissa said with a grin. "Do you have whipped cream?" she asked Matt.

"Coming up." He had it ready.

"A man after my own heart."

Matt couldn't help but glance at Noah. But Noah just grinned and rolled his eyes. He was clearly confident in his relationship. Matt couldn't help but feel a stab of jealousy. He couldn't remember ever being that content.

When Matt sat down, Noah rose.

"Before we start," Noah said.

"No." Melissa gave a mock whine.

"Hold tight," he said to her, giving her a squeeze on the shoulder.

Then he went to the refrigerator and produced the bottle of champagne he'd squirreled away.

"We need the right beverage for this." Noah presented the bottle.

"Oh, my favorite," Melissa said, clearly mollified by the offer of champagne.

Matt quickly moved to get six flutes from his cupboard.

"Nice," Caleb said. "What's the occasion?"

"Good friends," Noah said as he popped the cork. "Good family." He filled the flutes and Matt passed them around.

Then Matt sat down again.

Noah took Melissa's hand. He raised it and gave it a gentle kiss.

Something in his expression made her go still, and everyone went quiet along with her.

"You accepted me from minute one," he said to her. "All of you." He looked around at the group. "Every one of you welcomed me in, without judging, without suspicion."

"I judged a little," Caleb said.

Jules reached out to squeeze her husband's hand.

"You were protecting Jules," Noah said. "And you were protecting Melissa. And you were smart to do that with my history."

"You proved me wrong," Caleb said.

"I did. And now, I think, I hope…" Noah drew a deep breath. "Melissa, darling." His hand went to his pocket and extracted the ring box.

When she saw it, Melissa's eyes went round, and a flush came up on her cheeks.

Matt quickly reached for his phone, hitting the camera button.

Noah popped open the box. "Marry me?"

Melissa gasped. Jules squealed. And Matt got a fantastic picture of the moment.

Melissa's gaze went to the ring, and she leaned closer in. "It is absolutely gorgeous."

"Not as gorgeous as you."

She looked back to Noah. "Yes," she said. "Yes, yes, yes!"

His grin nearly split his face. Everyone cheered.

Her hand trembled as he slipped the ring on her finger. Then he drew her to her feet and kissed her, enveloping her in a sheltering hug. He looked like he'd never let her go.

Matt took one more shot, finding his chest tight, his thoughts going back to Tasha. He'd held her that tight and more last night. And, in the moment, he'd never wanted to let her go.

Tasha had to get away from Matt for a while. She needed to do something ordinary and find some perspective. Their lovemaking last night had tilted her universe, and she was desperate to get it back on an even keel.

She and Alex had taken a cab to the Edge tonight. They'd started with a couple of tequila shots and danced with a bunch of different guys. Then James Hamilton showed up and commandeered Alex for several dances in a row.

Tasha moved from partner to partner, and by the time she and Alex reconnected at the table, she was sweaty and on a second margarita. The drinks were bringing back memories of Matt, but she'd stopped caring.

James was talking to a couple of his friends across the room, leaving Alex alone with Tasha.

"So, are the two of you an item?" she asked Alex.

Alex shrugged. "I don't know. I like him. He seems to want to hang out a lot. Why?"

"Does it worry you?" Tasha asked. "Dating a mechanic. Do you think you'll lose your credibility? I always worried about dating someone in the business."

"It's a risk," Alex agreed, sipping some ice water through a straw. "But so far all we're doing is dancing."

"Oh." Tasha was surprised by that.

"You thought I was sleeping with James?"

"You left together the other night."

Alex laughed. "I wonder if that's what everybody thinks. And if it is…" She waggled her brows. "What's holding me back?"

Tasha felt terrible for making the assumption, worse for saying it out loud. "I didn't mean to judge, or to push you in any particular direction."

"You're not. You won't. You need to stop worrying so much. We're here to have fun."

"That's right. We are." Tasha lifted her drink in a toast.

As she clinked glasses with Alex, a man at the front door caught her attention. It was Matt. He walked in, and his gaze zeroed in on her with laser precision.

"No," she whispered under her breath.

"What?" Alex asked, leaning in to scrutinize her expression.

"Nothing. Do you mind if I dance with James?"

"Why would I mind? Go for it. I can use the rest."

Tasha slipped from the high stool at their compact round table. As Matt made his way toward her, she went off on an opposite tangent, heading straight for James.

"Dance?" she asked him brightly.

He looked a little surprised, but recovered quickly. "You bet." He took her hand.

The dance floor was crowded and vibrating, and she

quickly lost sight of Matt, throwing herself into the beat of the music.

The song ended too soon, and Matt cut in. James happily gave way.

"No," Tasha said to Matt as he tried to take her hand.

"No, what?"

"No, I don't want to do this."

The music was coming up, and she had to dance or look conspicuous out on the floor. She started to move, but kept a distance between them.

He closed the gap, enunciating above the music. "We're going to have to talk sometime."

She raised her voice to be heard. "What's the rush?"

"You'd rather let things build?"

"I was hoping they'd fade."

"My feelings aren't fading."

She glanced around, worried that people might overhear. The crowd was close, so she headed for the edge of the floor.

Matt followed.

When they got to a quieter corner, she spoke again. "Give it some time. We both need some space."

"Can you honestly say your feelings are fading?"

Her feelings weren't fading. They were intensifying.

"If nothing else, we work together," he said. "We have to interact to get our jobs done. And besides, beyond anything else, I'm worried about you."

"There's nothing to worry about." She paused. "Okay, but that thing is *you*."

"Very funny. I'm watching for anything unusual."

"So am I." She'd been working on the sabotage problem all night.

"What I'm seeing is a guy."

Her interest perked up. "At the pier?"

"Not there. Don't look right away, but he's over by the bar. He's been staring at you. And it looks odd. I mean, suspicious."

"What's that got to do with your yachts?"

"I don't know. Maybe nothing."

"Probably nothing. Almost certainly nothing."

"Turn slowly, pretend you're looking at the bottle display behind the bar, maybe picking out a brand. Then glance at the guy in the blue shirt with the black baseball cap. He's slouched at the second seat from the end."

"That sounds needlessly elaborate." She felt like she was in a spy movie.

"I want you to know what he looks like. In case he shows up somewhere else."

"This is silly."

"Humor me."

"Fine." She did as Matt suggested, focusing on the bottles, then doing a quick sweep of the guy Matt had described.

He looked like a perfectly normal fiftysomething, probably a little shy and nerdy sitting alone having a drink. He wasn't staring. He was likely people watching and just happened on Tasha when Matt walked in.

She turned back to Matt. "Okay, I saw him."

"Good. You need a drink?"

"I have a drink."

Matt looked at her hands.

The truth was Tasha didn't normally leave her drinks alone. She'd done it now because Matt had thrown her when he walked in. She hadn't been expecting him, and she'd taken the first opportunity to get out of his way. She might be in a low-risk environment, but it wasn't a risk she normally took.

"I'll get myself a new drink." She started for the bar,

hoping he'd stay behind. She'd come here to clear her head, avoid the memories of Matt's lovemaking. She had to focus, wanting to figure out whether the marina was in trouble…or maybe Matt was? The last thing she needed was to be distracted by his quick smile, broad chest and shoulders, his handsome face…

A tune blasted from the turntable, while voices of the crowd ebbed and flowed, laughter all around them under the festive lights. He fell into step beside her.

"I thought you were having dinner with Caleb and Jules," she said.

"Dinner ended early. Noah and Melissa got engaged."

Tasha was getting to know Melissa, and she'd met Noah a few times. "Noah proposed in front of everyone?"

"It was a daring move on Noah's part." Matt's gaze swept the room, obviously checking on the guy at the end of the bar. "I expect it left everybody feeling romantic, so they wanted to head home. Bit of a bummer for TJ. He fights it, but he's lonely. He liked being married."

"How did his wife die?" Tasha liked TJ. Her heart went out to him over the loss.

"Breast cancer."

"That's really sad."

"Yeah." Matt's voice was gruff. "It's been a tough haul. Let me get you that drink."

"I'm going to take off." She wanted to stay, but she needed to go. Clearing her head with Matt in front of her was impossible.

"We need to talk eventually."

"Later."

"I don't want you to be upset."

"I'm not. Actually, I'm not sure what I am."

He hesitated. "Okay. Fine. I don't want to push."

Relieved, she texted for a cab and let Alex know she was leaving. She knew it was the right thing to do, but she couldn't shake a hollow feeling as she headed for the parking lot.

Eight

When Tasha left the bar, the stranger left, too.

Matt followed him as far as the door, watching to be sure he didn't harass her in the parking lot. But she got immediately into a cab and left.

The stranger drove off a few minutes later in the opposite direction.

Back inside, Matt returned to the table to where Alex was now sitting.

"Hey, boss," she greeted with a smile.

"Having a good time?" he asked.

"You bet. Have you met James Hamilton?"

Matt shook the man's hand. "Good to meet you, James."

James nodded. "You, too."

Matt returned his attention to Alex. "Did you happen to notice if anyone was paying particular attention to Tasha tonight?"

Alex looked puzzled, but then shook her head. "She was dancing with lots of guys, but nobody in particular. A lot of them she knows from the area."

"Do you mean the old dude in the black cap?" James asked.

"Yes," Matt answered. "He was watching her the whole time I was here."

"Yeah. I noticed it most of the night. I don't know what his deal was. He never talked to her."

Alex looked to James. "Somebody was watching Tasha?"

"She's pretty hot," James said. "I just thought it was a bit of a creep factor. You know, because the guy was old. But he seemed harmless enough."

"He left when she left," Matt said.

James's gaze flicked to the door. "Did he give her any trouble?"

"No. I watched her get into a cab."

James gave a thoughtful nod.

"With everything that's going on at the marina..." Matt ventured.

"I know what you mean," Alex said. "It's happening more and more."

"What do you mean more and more?" Matt asked.

"Little things," Alex said. "Stupid things."

"Was there something besides the fuel leak and the electric short?"

"None worth getting excited about on their own. And we've checked the cameras. Nobody climbed the fence again."

"So a staff member? While you were open during the day?"

"It's possible. But I hear you've done at least ten background checks and didn't find anything."

Matt knew that was true.

"What's weird to me," Alex continued, "is that they're always on jobs done by Tasha."

Matt felt a prickle along his spine. "Are you sure about that?"

"Positive. We fix them. It doesn't take long."

"Why hasn't she said anything to me?" He'd hate to think the change in their personal relationship had made her reluctant to share information.

"She's starting to question her own memory. Any of them could have been mistakes. But any of them could have been on purpose, too."

"There's nothing wrong with her memory."

Tasha was smart, capable and thorough.

"I'm still wondering if it could be an inside job. I don't want to think that about any of my employees, but… As you're new to the team, has anyone struck you as suspicious?" A hand clapped down on Matt's shoulder.

He turned quickly, ready for anything. But it was TJ.

"Didn't know you were headed out, too," TJ said.

"I didn't know you hung out here," Matt responded, surprised to see his friend.

"I spotted your car in the lot. I was too restless to sleep. Hey, Alex." Then TJ turned his attention to James, holding out a hand. "TJ Bauer."

"I know who you are," James said.

"Really?"

"My mom's on the hospital auxiliary. I hear all about your generous donations."

Matt looked to TJ. He knew TJ's financial company made a number of charitable contributions. He hadn't realized they were noteworthy.

TJ waved the statement away. "It's a corporate thing. Most companies have a charitable arm."

"They were very excited to get the new CT scanner. So on behalf of my mom and the hospital, thank you."

"I better buy you a drink," Matt said to TJ.

"You'd better," TJ returned. "So, what's going on?"

"Some guy was watching Tasha all night long."

"Tasha's here?" TJ gazed around.

Matt couldn't seem to forget that TJ had been attracted to Tasha. Sure, it was mostly from afar, and sure, he'd promised to back off. Still, Matt couldn't help but be jealous.

"She left," he said.

"Too bad." Then TJ gave an unabashed grin and jostled Matt with his elbow.

Alex watched the exchange with obvious interest.

Matt braced himself, wishing he could shut TJ up.

But TJ was done. He drummed his hands against the wooden tabletop. "Is there a waiter or waitress around here?"

"I can go to the bar," James quickly offered.

"I'll come with," Alex said, sliding off the high stool.

"Whatever they have on tap," TJ said.

"Same for me," Matt said, sliding James a fifty. "Get yourselves something, too."

"Best boss in the world." Alex grinned.

"You know how to keep employees happy," TJ said as the pair walked away.

"I wish I knew how to keep one particular employee safe."

"You've got the new cameras now."

"Alex just told me there've been a couple of other minor incidents that looked like tampering. Tasha didn't say anything to me about them." Matt was definitely going to bring that up with her. He wished he could do it now. He didn't want to wait until morning.

"She probably didn't want you going all white knight on her."

"I don't do that."

"You like her, bro."

Matt wasn't about to deny it.

"And you worry about her. And she strikes me as the self-sufficient type."

"She is that," Matt agreed. "But she knows we're all looking to find this guy. Why would she withhold information?"

"Ask her."

"I will. The other thing Alex said was the weird things only happened after Tasha had done a repair, not when it was Alex or anyone else. And this guy watching her tonight? That makes me even more curious." Matt hated to think Tasha might be some kind of target in all this.

"It seems unlikely tonight's guy is related to the sabotage," TJ said.

"He followed her out."

"Probably working up his nerve to ask her on a date."

Matt scoffed at that. "He was twice her age."

"Some guys still think they have a shot. And he doesn't know he'd have to go through you to get to her."

Matt didn't respond. He didn't usually keep things from his friend, but he had no intention of telling TJ how far things had gone with Tasha. "I'm worried about her."

"Worry away. Just don't do anything outrageous."

Like sleeping with her? "Like what?"

"Like locking her up in a tower."

Despite his worry, Matt couldn't help but smile at that. "My place does have a great security system."

TJ chuckled. "Now *that* would be an example of what not to do."

"I won't." But there were a dozen reasons why Matt would love to lock her away in his house and keep her all to himself.

* * *

As the sun rose in the early morning, Tasha made her way up from the compact engine room into the bridge and living quarters of the yacht *Crystal Zone*. Between reliving her lovemaking with Matt and worrying about the sabotage, she'd barely been able to sleep. After tossing and turning most of the night, an early start had seemed like the most productive solution.

Now, she came to the top of the stairs in the yacht's main living area, and a sixth sense made her scalp tingle. She froze. She looked around, but nothing seemed out of place. She listened, hearing only the lapping of the waves and the creak of the ship against the pier.

Still, she couldn't shake the unsettling feeling. She wrinkled her nose and realized it was a scent. There was an odd scent in the room. It seemed familiar, yet out of place. She tried to make herself move, but she couldn't get her legs to cooperate.

She ordered herself to quit freaking out. Everything was fine with the engine. It was in better shape than ever, since she kept fussing with it. The door to the rear deck was closed. Dawn had broken, and she could see through the window that nobody was outside.

Nobody was watching her.

She forced herself to take a step forward, walking on the cardboard stripping that covered the polished floor to protect it from grease and oil. *Crystal Zone* was going out today on a six-day run.

Then she heard a sound.

She stopped dead.

It came again.

Somebody was on the forward deck. The outer door creaked open. She grabbed for the biggest wrench in her tool belt, sliding it out. If this was someone up to no good, they were going to have a fight on their hands.

She gripped the wrench tightly, moving stealthily forward.

"Matt?" a man's voice called out.

It was Caleb.

Her knees nearly gave way with relief. Nobody had broken in. Caleb had the gate code and was obviously looking for Matt.

She swallowed, reclaiming her voice. "It's Tasha. I'm in here."

"Tasha?" Caleb appeared on the bridge. "Is Matt with you?"

"He's not here."

"I saw the light was on. Why are you starting so early?" Caleb glanced at his watch.

"Couldn't sleep," she said, her stomach relaxing. She slid the wrench back into the loop.

"Way too much going on," he said with understanding.

"I heard Melissa and Noah got engaged."

"They did. It was pretty great." Caleb moved farther into the living area. "Did Matt tell you Melissa and Jules are determined to decorate his place for the holidays?"

"I'm sure he appreciates it."

Caleb chuckled. "I'm sure he doesn't. Dianne was big on decorating."

"Oh."

"I heard you met her." Caleb seemed to be fishing for something.

"I did."

"How did it go?"

Tasha couldn't help remembering her last conversation with Dianne. "I'm not sure. She seems…sad."

The answer obviously surprised Caleb. "Sad? Dianne?"

Tasha weighed the wisdom of taking this chance to ask Caleb directly about a job. She didn't want to put him on the spot.

Then again, she didn't know him very well, so he could easily turn her down without hurting her feelings.

"Can I ask you something?" she asked.

He looked curious. "Fire away."

"I know you have Neo restaurant locations all over the country."

"We have a few."

"Dianne is in pretty dire straits. She's lost everything."

Caleb's expression hardened a shade, but Tasha forced herself to go on.

"She has no money. And she needs a job. I think she's pretty desperate."

"She snowed you," Caleb said, tone flat.

"That doesn't seem true. She didn't know I was there. And she was pretty obviously distraught. Also, she doesn't strike me as somebody whose first plan of attack would be to seek employment."

"You've got that right. She likely hasn't worked a day in her life."

"She admits she doesn't have a lot of marketable skills. But she said she can host parties. She's attractive, articulate, refined."

"What are you getting at?"

"Maybe a hostess position or special events planner somewhere…not here, maybe on the eastern seaboard?"

"Ah." A look of comprehension came over Caleb's face. "Get her out of Matt's hair."

"Well, that, and give her a chance at building a life. If

she's telling the truth, and she definitely seemed sincere, she has absolutely nothing left and nowhere to turn."

"It's her own fault," Caleb said.

"No argument from me. But everybody makes mistakes."

He paused, seeming to consider the point. "I know I've made enough of them." He seemed to be speaking half to himself.

"Will you think about it?" Tasha dared to press.

"I'll see what I can do. I suppose it's the season to do the right thing."

"It is."

Light rain drizzled down from the gray clouds above, the temperature hovering in the fifties. It hadn't snowed this year. Snow was always a rare event in this pocket of the coast, and the last white Christmas had been ten years back.

"If you come across Matt, will you tell him I'm looking for him?" Caleb was probably regretting his decision to check inside *Crystal Zone*.

"Anything I can help you with?" she asked.

"Nope. I just want to warn him that Jules and Melissa are going shopping today for holiday decorations. He better brace himself to look festive."

Tasha couldn't stop a smile. "I'll tell him."

"Thanks."

"No, thank you. Seriously, Caleb, thank you for helping Dianne."

"I haven't done anything yet."

"But you're going to try."

He turned to leave, but then braced a hand on the stairway, turning back. "You do know this isn't your problem."

"I know. But it's hard when you don't have a family. People to support you."

He hesitated. "You don't have a family?"

"Estranged. It's lonely at times."

"Same with me," he said. "But my wife, Jules, Melissa, Noah, TJ, they're good people, I've found a family here. I bet you have, too."

"Soon you'll have two more members in your new family."

Caleb broke into a wide smile. "You got that right. See you, Tasha."

"Goodbye, Caleb."

The sun was now up, and Tasha's feeling of uneasiness had completely faded. She was glad she'd asked Caleb about the job directly. It was better than dragging Jules into the middle of it.

Tasha gathered up the rest of her tools, turned off the lights and secured the doors. She'd head to the main building and get cleaned up before she started on the next job. Alex would probably be in by now, and they could plan the details of their day.

Out on the pier, she shifted the toolbox to her right hand and started to make her way to shore. Almost immediately she saw Matt coming the other way.

His shoulders were square, his stride determined and his chin was held high. She wondered if he'd found some information on the saboteur.

"Morning," she called out as she grew closer.

He didn't smile.

"Did something happen?" She reflexively checked out the remaining row of yachts. She didn't see anything out of place.

"I just talked to Caleb."

"Oh, good. He was looking for you." She struggled to figure out why Matt was frowning.

"You asked him about Dianne." The anger in Matt's tone was clear.

"I..." She'd known it was a risk. She shouldn't be surprised by his anger. "I only asked if he could help."

"Without even *telling* me, you asked my best friend to give my ex-wife a job?"

When he put it that way, it didn't sound very good.

"Only if he didn't mind," she said.

"You don't think that was unfair to him? What if he doesn't want to hire her? Heck, I'm not sure I'd want to hire her."

"Then he can say no. It was a question. He has a choice."

"You put him in an impossible situation."

"Matt, I know it was a bad divorce. Dianne might not be the greatest person in the world. But she is a person. And she is in trouble."

"She got herself into it."

"She made a mistake. She knows that."

Tasha set down the toolbox. It was growing heavy. "You can give her a break, Matt. Everybody deserves a break at some point."

"There's such a thing as justice."

"It seems she's experienced justice and then some."

"You don't know her."

"She can't be all bad. You married her. You must have loved her at some point, right?"

The question seemed to give him pause. The wind whipped his short hair, and the salt spray misted over them.

"I'm not sure I ever did," he finally said.

"What?" Tasha couldn't imagine marrying anyone she didn't love. She would never marry someone she didn't love.

"I didn't see her clearly at first. It seemed like we wanted the same things out of life."

The admission shouldn't have taken her by surprise. Matt had never made a secret of the fact that he wanted wealth, status and luxury.

"Don't be like them," she said.

He looked confused. "Like Dianne? I'm not like Dianne. I've worked hard for everything I've earned, and I appreciate it and don't take it for granted."

"I know." She did. "What I mean is, don't turn into one of those callous elites, forgetting about the day-to-day struggles of ordinary people."

"Except that Dianne is calculating."

"She needs a job."

"She does. But all she's ever aspired to is a free ride."

"Desperation is a powerful motivator. And Caleb can always fire her."

Matt clamped his jaw. "You shouldn't have interfered."

"Maybe not." She couldn't entirely disagree. "I felt sorry for her."

"Because you're too trusting."

Tasha didn't think that was true, but she wasn't going to argue anymore. She'd done what she'd done, and he had every right to be upset. "I have to meet Alex now."

"Right." He looked like he wanted to say more. "I'll catch you later."

"Sure." At this point, she had her doubts that he'd try.

Matt entered the Crab Shack after the lunch rush to find Caleb at the bar talking with his sister-in-law, Melissa.

He knew he couldn't let this morning's argument sit. He had to address it right away.

He stopped in front of Caleb, bracing himself. "I didn't mean to jump down your throat this morning."

"Not a problem," Caleb easily replied.

From behind the bar, Melissa poured them each an ice water and excused herself.

"I was shocked is all," Matt said. "Tasha put you in an awkward situation. I should have made it clear right then that I didn't want you to do it."

"It's already done."

"What?"

Caleb stirred the ice water with the straw. "Dianne has a job at the Phoenix Neo and a plane ticket to get there."

"You didn't. Why would you do that? We didn't even finish our conversation."

"I didn't do it for you, Matt. I did it for Dianne. I did it for everyone."

"She probably won't work out."

"Maybe, maybe not."

"She needs to face the results of her own actions. It's not up to you to rescue her."

"I didn't rescue her. I gave her a shot. She's lost her fortune. She's lost you. She's lost that guy she thought was going to be her Prince Charming. It's not up to me, you're right. It's up to her. She'll make it at Neo or she won't, just like any other employee we've ever hired."

Matt hated to admit it, but Caleb was making good points. Dianne was on her own now. And she'd have to work if she wanted to succeed. There was justice in that.

"And she's in Phoenix," Caleb finished. "She's not here."

"I suppose I should thank you for that," Matt said. He took a big swallow of the water. Not having to see Dianne, frankly, was a huge relief.

"You bet you should thank me for that. And that's what friends do, by the way."

"There's a fire!" Melissa suddenly cried from the opposite side of the restaurant. "Oh, Matt, it looks like one of your boats!"

Matt dropped his glass on the bar and rushed across the room. Smoke billowed up from the far end of the pier. He couldn't tell which yacht was on fire, but all he could think of was Tasha. Where was Tasha?

"Call 911," he yelled to Melissa as he sprinted for the door.

He jumped into his car. Caleb clambered in beside him. Caleb barely got the door shut, and Matt was peeling from the parking lot.

"Can you tell what's on fire?" he asked Caleb as they sped along the spit of land that housed the Crab Shack.

"It has to be a boat. *Orca's Run* is blocking the view. But I don't think it's the one on fire."

"How the hell did he do it?" Matt gripped the steering wheel, sliding around the corner at the shoreline, heading for the pier. "If it's a stranger, how did he get to another one? Everyone's been on the lookout."

"I can see flames," Caleb said. "It's bad."

"Can you see people? Tasha?"

"There are people running down the pier. I can't tell who is who."

It felt like an eternity before Matt hit the parking lot. He slammed on the brakes, but it was still a run to get to the pier. The gate was open, and he sprinted through. "Grab the hoses," he called to the deckhands and maintenance crews. Could it be one of them? Was it possible that someone on the inside had actually set a boat on fire? "Start the pumps!"

The staff drilled for fires. At full deployment, their

equipment could pump over a hundred gallons a minute from the ocean.

It was the fifty-foot *Crystal Zone* that was on fire. The entire cabin was engulfed in flames, and they were threatening the smaller craft, *Never Fear*, that was moored directly behind on a floater jutting out from the pier.

He looked behind him to see three crew members lugging lengths of fire hose. Caleb was helping them. But Matt didn't see Tasha. Where was Tasha?

And then he saw her. She was climbing onto the deck of *Salty Sea*, which was in the berth next to *Crystal Zone*. It was barely ten feet away from the flames. There were clients on that boat, two families due to leave port in a couple of hours. The smoke was thick, and she quickly disappeared into it.

Matt increased his speed, running up the gangway to the deck of *Salty Sea*.

"Tasha!" His lungs filled with smoke, and he quickly ducked to breathe cleaner air.

And then he saw her. She was shepherding a mother and two children toward the gangway.

"Five more," she called out harshly as she passed him.

He wanted to grab her. He wanted to hug her. He wanted to reassure himself that she was okay. But he knew it would have to wait. The passengers needed his help.

Eyes watering, he pressed on toward the cabin.

There he met one of the dads, the other mother and the remaining two children.

"Follow me," he rasped, picking up the smallest child.

They made it quickly to the gangway, where the air was clear.

"We're missing one," Tasha said, starting back.

"Stay here!" he told her.

She ignored him, pushing back into the smoke.

Together, they found the last man. He was on the top deck, and Matt guided him to a ladder. They quickly got him to the gangway, and he made his way down.

Matt took a second to survey the disastrous scene.

Neither he nor Tasha said a word.

Caleb and the workers were connecting the lengths of hose.

Alex was preparing the pump.

His gaze went to *Crystal Zone*. She was a complete loss, and *Never Fear* was next. It was too far away from the pier. The spray wouldn't reach it.

Then Matt heard it or smelled it or felt it.

"Get down!" he shouted, grabbing Tasha and throwing her to the deck, covering her body with his and closing his eyes tight.

Never Fear's gasoline tanks exploded. The boom echoing in his ears, the shock wave and heat rushed over him. People on the dock roared in fear.

While debris rained down on him and Tasha, and his ears rang from the boom, Matt gave a frantic look to the people on the pier.

Some had been knocked down, but *Crystal Zone* had blocked most of the blast. He and Tasha had taken the brunt.

"We're good," Caleb called out to him, rushing from person to person. "We're all good."

Matt watched a moment longer before looking to Tasha beneath him.

"Are you hurt?" he asked her.

She shook her head. Then she coughed. When she spoke, her voice was strangled. "I'm fine." She paused. "Oh, Matt."

"I know," he said.

—

"I don't understand. Who would do this? People could have been killed."

"Yeah," he agreed, coughing himself. He eased off her. "Can you move?"

"Yes." She came to her knees.

He did the same.

She looked around. "You've lost two boats."

"Maybe three." *Salty Sea* was also damaged, its windows blown out from the blast.

Sirens sounded in the distance as the fire department made its way down the cliff road.

Matt took Tasha's hand. "We need to get off here. It's going to catch, too."

She came shakily to her feet.

Caleb met them at the bottom of the gangway.

Alex had the pumps running, and the crew was spraying water on the flames.

The fire engine stopped in the parking lot, and the firefighters geared up, heading down the pier on foot.

Matt turned Tasha to face him, taking in every inch of her. "Are you sure you're all right?"

"You're hurt," she said, pointing to his shoulder.

"You're bleeding," Caleb told him.

"It feels fine." Matt didn't feel a thing.

"You'll need stitches," she said.

"There'll be a medic here in a few minutes. They can bandage me up."

Looking around, it seemed Matt's was the only injury. He'd have plenty of attention. And his shoulder didn't hurt yet.

"Thank you." Tasha's low voice was shaking.

He wrapped an arm around her shoulders. "You probably saved their lives." If she hadn't got everyone out of the cabin, they would have been caught in the blast.

"You, too."

He drew a deep breath and coughed some more.

"The media is here," Caleb said.

Matt realized publicity was inevitable. "I'll talk to them in a minute."

"Are you going to tell them about the sabotage?" Tasha asked.

"No. It's better that we keep that quiet for now."

"I checked *Crystal Zone* this morning. There was no reason in the world for it to catch fire." A funny expression came over her face.

"What is it?"

Her eyes narrowed.

"Tasha?"

"You're going to think I'm nuts."

"Whatever it is, tell me."

"When I came up from the engine room, I got this creepy feeling, a sixth-sense thing. It felt like somebody was watching me. But then Caleb showed up, and I thought he was the reason."

Fear flashed through Matt. "Somebody else was on the boat with you? Did you see who?"

"I didn't. I mean, besides Caleb. But now…"

"Mr. Emerson?" A reporter shoved a microphone in front of him.

Someone else snapped a picture.

He nudged Tasha to leave. She didn't need to face this.

He'd get it over with, answer their questions, get the fire out and then sit down and figure out what on earth was going on.

Nine

For the first time, Tasha wished her room in the staff quarters had a bathtub. She was usually content with a quick shower. Getting clean was her objective, not soaking in foamy or scented water.

But tonight, she'd have given a lot for the huge soaker tub from her old bathroom in Boston. She shampooed her hair a second time, trying to remove the smoke smell. She scrubbed her skin, finding bumps and bruises. And when she started to shake, she reminded herself that she was fine, Matt was fine, everybody was thankfully fine.

The police were getting involved now, so surely they'd get to the bottom of the inexplicable sabotage. Matt had said, and she agreed, this went far beyond what any of his competitors would do to gain a business advantage. So unless something had gone catastrophically wrong in an unplanned way today, they were looking for a much more sinister motive.

The firefighters had said the blaze had started in the engine room, identifying it as the source of the fire. They expected to know more specifics in the next few days.

She shut off the taps, wrapped a towel around her hair,

dried her skin and shrugged into her terry-cloth robe. It was only eight in the evening, but she was going to bed. Maybe she'd read a while to calm her mind. But she was exhausted. And tomorrow was going to be another overwhelming day.

A knock sounded on her door, startling her. Adrenaline rushed her system, and her heart thudded in her chest. It was silly to be frightened. She was not going to be frightened.

"Tasha?" It was Matt.

"Yes?"

He waited a moment. "Can you open the door?"

She almost said she wasn't dressed. But the man had already seen her naked. The bathrobe, by comparison, was overdressed. She tightened the sash and unlocked the door, pulling it open.

"Hey," he said, his blue eyes gentle.

She fought an urge to walk into his arms. "Hi."

"How are you feeling?"

"I'll be fine."

"I didn't ask what you'd be. I asked how you are." He looked solid and strong, like a hug from him would be exactly the reassurance she needed right now.

But she had to be strong herself. "Sore." It was a truthful answer without going into her state of mind. "You?"

"Yeah. Pretty sore." He gestured into the room.

She stepped aside. It felt reassuring to have him here. It was good to have his company.

He closed the door and leaned back against it. "I don't think you're safe."

She was jumpy. But she knew it was a natural reaction to being so close to an explosion. She'd be fine after a good night's sleep.

"I'm okay," she said.

He eased a little closer. "We agree this wasn't a competitor. And if it's not Whiskey Bay Marina—and it's likely *not* Whiskey Bay Marina—then the next logical guess is you."

"That doesn't make sense." She couldn't wrap her mind around someone, *anyone*, targeting her.

"I'm afraid for you, Tasha."

"We don't know—"

He moved closer still. "I don't care what we know and don't know."

"Matt."

He took her hands in his. "Listen to me."

"This is wild speculation."

She tried to ignore his touch. But it felt good. It felt right. It felt more comforting than made sense. She prided herself on her independence, and here she was wishing she could lean on Matt.

"Somebody's targeted you," he said. "Somebody who's willing to commit arson and harm people."

"Why would they do that to me? Who would do that to me?"

"I don't know. All I do know is that it's happening, and you need protection. I want to do that, Tasha. I want to protect you." He squeezed her hands. "I couldn't live with myself if anything happened to you."

"You're blowing this out of proportion, Matt."

He crossed the last inches between them, and his arms brushed hers. "They set a boat on fire."

She didn't have a response for that.

"I want you to stay at the main house."

"You mean your house." That was a dangerous idea. It was a frightening idea. Just standing so close to him now, her emotions were swinging off-kilter.

"I have an alarm system. I have good locks on my doors. And I'm there. I'm *there* if anything goes wrong."

"It's nice of you to offer," she said, her logical self at odds with the roller coaster of her emotions.

She couldn't stay under the same roof as Matt, not with her feelings about him so confused, not with her attraction to him so strong, and certainly not right out there in front of the entire staff and crew of the marina.

"I am your boss, and as a condition of your employment, you need to stay safe, Tasha."

"You *know* what people will think." She grasped at a perfectly logical argument. No way, no how was she going to admit she didn't trust herself with him.

"I couldn't care less what people will think."

"I do. I care."

"Do you want a chaperone? Should we ask someone to come stay there with us?"

"That would make it look even worse."

He drew back a little and gently let her hands go, seeming to give her some space.

"I have a guest room. This is about security and nothing more. Everybody here knows you. If you don't make a big deal about the arrangement, neither will they. The police are involved. There's a serious criminal out there, and it has something to do with you."

She closed her eyes for a long second, steeling herself, telling herself she could handle it. She had control of her emotions.

He was right, and she needed to make the best of it. She'd go stay behind his locks and his alarm system. She'd be practical. She could keep her distance. And she'd keep it light.

"Do you have a soaker tub?" she joked, wincing at her sore muscles.

He gave a ghost of a smile. “Yes, I do. Get your things.”

She moved to the closet where she had a gym bag, feeling every muscle involved. “I feel like I’ve been in a bar fight.”

“Have you been in many bar fights?”

“Have you?” she countered.

“A couple. And, yeah, this is pretty much what it feels like.”

Having accepted the inevitable, Tasha tossed some necessities into her gym bag, changed in the bathroom and was ready in a few minutes.

“You’re frighteningly fast at that,” Matt noted as they stepped onto the porch.

“I’m leaving my ball gowns behind.”

“Are you going to lock it?” he asked, looking pointedly at the door.

“There’s not much inside.”

“With all that’s going on?” He raised his brow.

“Fine. You’re right. It’s the smart thing to do.” She dug into the pocket of her pants, found the key and turned it in the lock.

He lifted her bag from her hand. She would have protested, but it seemed like too much trouble. It was only a five-minute climb to the front door of his house. She couldn’t bring herself to worry about which one of them carried her bag.

Inside Matt’s house, boxes and bags littered the entryway. There were more of them in the living room, stacked on the coffee table and on the sofa and chairs.

“You did a little shopping?” she asked, relieved to have something to be amused about.

“Jules and Melissa. They were going to decorate tonight. But, well…maybe tomorrow.”

"Maybe," Tasha echoed.

It was less than two weeks until Christmas, but she couldn't imagine Matt was feeling very much like celebrating the season.

He set her bag down at the end of the hall. "Thirsty?"

"Yes." She found a vacant spot on the sofa and sat down.

If Matt wanted to bring her a drink, she wasn't about to argue. He went into the kitchen, opening cupboards and sliding drawers.

Curious, she leaned forward to look inside one of the shopping bags. Wrapped in tissue paper were three porcelain snowmen with smiling faces, checkerboard scarves and top hats. They were adorable.

She spied a long, narrow white shelf suspended above the fireplace. It was sparsely decorated, so she set the snowmen up at one end.

"There's no way to stop this, is there?" Matt gazed in resignation at the snowmen.

"You don't like them?" She was disappointed.

"No. They're cute. They're different. Different is good." He had a glass of amber liquid in cach hand. It was obvious from their balloon shape that he'd poured some kind of brandy.

"This is your first Christmas since the divorce." It wasn't a question. It was an observation.

"It is." He handed her one of the glasses. "Caleb gave Dianne a job in Phoenix thanks to you."

Tasha wasn't sure how to respond. She couldn't tell from Matt's tone if he was still angry. "We aren't going to fight again, are we?"

"No. I hope not. Too much else has happened."

She returned to the sofa and took a sip of the brandy.

"This is delicious," she said.

He took the only vacant armchair. "A gift from Caleb. He's more of a connoisseur than I am."

"He has good taste."

Matt raised his glass. "To Caleb's good taste."

She lifted her own. "Thank you, Caleb."

Matt sighed, leaned back in the soft chair and closed his eyes.

Tasha felt self-conscious, as if she'd intruded on his life.

She gazed at his handsome face for a few more minutes. Then her attention drifted to the glass walls, to the extraordinary view of the bay and the marina. The Neo restaurant was well under way. The job site was lit at night, a few people still working. She could see the flash of a welder and the outline of a crane against the steel frame of the building.

The yachts bobbed on the tides, a gaping black hole where the fire had burned. *Crystal Zone* hadn't been the finest in the fleet, but it was a favorite of Tasha's. She was going to miss working on it.

"You're going to have to help me," Matt said.

"Help you with what?"

He opened his eyes. "Buy a new boat. Make that two new boats."

"You'll be able to repair *Salty Sea*?"

"I think so. We'll have to strip it down, but it's not a total write-off. *Never Fear* is mostly debris at the bottom of the bay."

"Ironic that," she said.

"In what way?"

"We should have feared her."

Matt smiled. Then he took another sip of his brandy.

She set down her glass and looked into another of the shopping bags. This one contained cylindrical glass containers, stubby candles, glass beads and a bag of cranberries.

"I know exactly what to do with these," she said.

"Here we go." He sat up straighter.

She opened the bag of glass beads, slowly pouring a layer into each of the two containers. "Do you mind if I put this together?"

"Please do."

She set the candles inside, positioning them straight. Then she poured a layer of cranberries around them, finishing off with more glass beads.

While she worked, Matt rose and removed the bags from the coffee table, the sofa and elsewhere, and gathered them off to the side of the room. He positioned her finished creations in the center of the table and retrieved a long butane lighter from above the fireplace.

"You're not going to save them for Christmas?"

"I'm sure we can get more candles." He touched the lighter's flame to each wick. Lastly, he dimmed the lights. "This is nice."

When he moved past her, his shoulder touching hers, her nerve endings came to attention. He paused, and the warmth of his body seemed to permeate her skin.

She drew a deep breath, inhaling his scent. A part of her acknowledged that this was exactly what she'd feared and reminded herself she needed to fight it. Another part of her wanted the moment to go on forever.

"I'm glad you're here," he said in a soft tone.

It took a second to find her voice. She forced herself to keep it light. "Because you need help decorating?"

He didn't answer right away. When he did, he sounded disappointed. "Right. That's the reason."

She gave herself an extra couple of seconds, and then she eased away.

He seemed to take the hint and moved back to his chair.

She shook her emotions back to some semblance of normal. "So that's it?" She looked pointedly at the rest of the bags. "We're giving up on the decorating?"

"We're resting." He sounded normal again. "It's been a long day."

"Well, I'm curious now." It felt like there were unopened presents just waiting for her to dig in.

He gave a helpless shrug and a smile. "Go for it."

Tasha dug into a few more bags. She put silver stylized trees on the end tables, a basket of pinecones and red balls next to the candles. She hung two silver and snowflake-printed stockings above the fire, and wrestled a bent willow reindeer out of its box to set it up on the floor beside the fireplace.

When she discovered the components of an artificial tree, Matt gave up watching and rose to help.

"I knew you'd cave," she told him with a teasing smile.

"It says on the box that it's ten feet high. You'll never get it up by yourself."

"Oh, ye of little faith."

"Oh, ye of little height."

She laughed, amazed that she could do that at the end of such a trying day.

Together, they read the directions and fit the various pieces together, eventually ending up with a ten-foot balsam fir standing majestically in the center of the front window.

They both stood back to admire their work.

"Is that enough for tonight?" he asked.

"It's enough for tonight."

She felt an overwhelming urge to hug him. She wanted

to thank him for helping with the tree. She wanted to thank him for saving her from the explosion.

More than that, she wanted to kiss him and make love to him and spend the night in his arms. Her feelings were dangerous. She had to control them.

Steeling herself, she stepped away. "Okay to finish my brandy in the tub?"

His gaze sizzled on her for a moment.

"Alone," she said.

"I know."

She forced her feet to move.

Matt shouldn't have been surprised to find Tasha gone when he went into the kitchen for breakfast. She'd probably left early, hoping nobody would notice she hadn't slept in the staff quarters.

He wanted to text her to make sure she was all right. But he settled for staring out the window as he sipped his coffee, waiting until he spotted her on the pier with Alex. Only then did he pop a bagel in the toaster and check the news.

As expected, the fire was front and center in the local and state news. But he was surprised to see the article displayed prominently on a national site. He supposed the combination of fire, high-end yachts and an explosion, especially when there were pictures, was pretty hard to resist. They showed a shot of him and Tasha coming off *Salty Sea* after the explosion, side by side with a still photo of the crews fighting the flames.

He had planned to work at home this morning, as he normally did. But he was going down to the office instead. He wanted to be close to Tasha in case anything more happened.

Before he could leave, Jules and Melissa came by, calling out from the entryway.

"In the kitchen," he called back.

Jules spoke up. "We came to see how you were doing." She paused before coming down the four steps into the main living area. "And to see how you liked the decorations." She continued into the living room and gestured around. "Hey, you really got into the spirit."

"I did."

"Nice work." Melissa gazed around approvingly.

He knew he should credit Tasha. And he knew it wouldn't stay secret that she was sleeping here. But he wasn't in a rush to share the information. There was enough going on today.

"The insurance adjustors will be here at noon," he said instead.

"That's fast."

"I need to get things under way." If he was going to replace the boats before the spring season, he had no time to lose.

"Good thing it's the off-season," Melissa said, obviously following his train of thought.

"If there's anything to be grateful for, that's it. And that nobody got hurt." He was grateful for both things, but he wasn't going to relax until the perpetrator was caught and put in jail.

TJ was next through the door.

"How're you doing?" he asked Matt, giving Jules and Melissa each a nod.

"Fine." Matt thought about his conversation with Tasha last night, and he couldn't help but smile. "A bit like I've been in a bar fight."

TJ grinned back. "My guess is that two of the yachts are write-offs?"

"I'll confirm that today. But, I can't see how we save either of them."

"If you need interim financing, just let me know."

It was on the tip of Matt's tongue to refuse. He hated to take advantage of his friends. And he was already one favor down because of Caleb hiring Dianne.

But he had to be practical. TJ had access to almost unlimited funds. Matt would cover any interest payments. And having TJ write a check, instead of explaining the situation to a banker, would definitely speed things up.

"I might," he said to TJ. "I'm going to track down replacements just as soon as I can make some appointments."

"New yachts," Melissa said with a grin. "Now, *that's* what I call a Christmas gift."

"You can help me test them out," Matt offered.

"I'm your girl," she said.

Matt retrieved his cup and took the final swallow of his coffee. "Thanks for checking on me, guys. But I have to get to work."

"We'll get out of your way," Jules said.

"Nice job with the decorating," Melissa said as they turned to leave.

"I thought we were going to have to do it all," Jules said to her sister as they headed through the foyer.

As the door closed behind Jules and Melissa, TJ looked pointedly around the room. "What is with all this?"

"Tasha helped," Matt said.

"Last night?" TJ asked, his interest obviously perking up.

"I wanted her safely surrounded by an alarm system."

"So, it wasn't..."

"She slept in the guest room."

"Too bad."

"Seriously? She was nearly blown up yesterday. So were we."

"And you couldn't find it in your heart to comfort her?"

Matt knew it was a joke. TJ was absolutely not the kind of guy who would take advantage of a woman's emotional state.

"Is she staying again tonight?" TJ asked.

"Until we catch the jerk that did this. Yes, she's staying right here. I wish I hadn't committed to the mayor's party this evening."

"I could hang out with her."

Since TJ had once asked Tasha on a date, Matt wasn't crazy about that idea.

TJ put on an affronted expression. "You honestly think I'd make a move on her?"

"Of course not."

"Take her with you," TJ suggested.

"She hates those kinds of parties." It was too bad. Matt would happily keep her by his side.

"Everybody hates those kinds of parties."

"I don't."

"Then there's something wrong with you."

Matt didn't think there was anything wrong with him. There were a lot of positives to his hard work, and socializing was one of them. He employed nearly fifty people. He brought economic activity to Whiskey Bay, a town he loved.

And he liked the people of Whiskey Bay. He liked discussing issues with them. He liked strategizing with the other business owners, and he sure didn't mind doing it in a gracious setting.

"The food's good. The drinks are good. I like the music, and the company is usually pleasant. Plus tonight.

Tonight everyone will want to talk about the fire. And I can use that as a way to pump them all for information. You never know what people might have seen or heard around town."

"Tell that to Tasha," TJ said.

Matt paused to think about that. He had to admit it was a good idea. "She was willing to come along last time when it was part of the investigation."

"Keeps her with you."

"She's a pretty skilled interrogator. You know, for somebody who hates those kinds of parties, she handles them beautifully. Did you know she grew up in Boston? Beacon Hill. She can hobnob with the best of them. And she's totally disarming. She's pretty, smart and funny. Easy to talk to. Trustworthy. People will tell her anything. It's perfect."

Matt stopped talking to find TJ staring quizzically at him.

"You do get what's going on here, right?" TJ asked.

"No." Did TJ know something about the saboteur? "Did you hear something? Did you see something? Why didn't you *say* something?"

"You're falling in love with Tasha."

Matt shook his head to get the astonishment out. "I thought you were talking about the fire."

"Mark my words."

"You're about a thousand steps ahead of yourself."

Being attracted to a woman didn't equate to happily-ever-after. Sure, he was incredibly attracted to Tasha. And he'd admit to himself that it wasn't simply physical. Although mostly what they did was argue. And they'd slept together exactly *one* time. TJ didn't even know about that.

Matt was miles away from thinking about love.

"I can read the signs," TJ said.

"Well, you're getting a false reading. And I'm going to work now." Matt started for his front door.

TJ trailed behind. "Better brace yourself, buddy. Because I *can* read the signs."

Officially, Tasha agreed to attend the mayor's party because she could talk to people, see if anybody knew anything. If the price for that was dancing with Matt, so be it.

Anticipation brought a smile to her face as she got ready for the evening.

Tasha quickly found a dress she liked in Matt's basement. Sleeveless, with a short, full skirt, it was made of shimmering champagne tulle. The outer dress was trimmed and decorated with hand-stitched lace, and the underdress was soft satin. Altogether, it was made for dancing.

A pair of shoes and the small clutch purse in a box below had obviously been bought to match the dress. The shoes were definitely not made for dancing, but Tasha was going to wear them anyway. Her more practical side protested the frivolous decision. But she wanted to look beautiful tonight.

She wanted to look beautiful for Matt.

She paused for a moment to let the thought sink in.

She had at first chosen a basic black dress from the rack. There was nothing wrong with it. It was understated but perfectly acceptable. Black wasn't exactly her color. But it was a safe choice.

"Tasha?" Matt called from the hallway.

"Yes?" she called back.

"We've got about twenty minutes, and then we should get going."

"No problem." But then she'd spotted a champagne-colored gown and it had held her attention. She'd left with both dresses, and she glanced from one to the other now. Letting out a deep breath, she plucked the champagne-colored one from the hanger. She couldn't help feeling like one of her sisters, primping for a fancy party in the hopes of impressing a rich man.

She'd never understood it before, and she didn't want to understand it now. But she did. She couldn't help herself. She wanted Matt to see her as beautiful.

She set the dress on the bed and shoes on the floor. The guest bathroom was spacious and opulent. Her few toiletries took up only a tiny corner of the vanity.

She stripped off her clothes, noting small bruises on her elbow and her shoulder. She was feeling a lot better than yesterday, but she was still sore. Her gaze strayed to the huge soaker tub next to the walk-in shower. She promised herself she'd take advantage of it later.

For now, she twisted her hair into a braided updo, brushed her teeth, put on some makeup and shimmied into the dress. She didn't have much in the way of jewelry, but she did have a little pair of emerald-and-diamond studs that her parents had given her for her eighteenth birthday.

The last thing she put on was the shoes. They weren't a perfect fit, but they did look terrific. She popped her phone and a credit card into the purse, and headed out to meet Matt.

His bedroom door was open, and the room was empty, as was the living room. Then she heard movement at the front door. Feeling guilty for having kept him waiting, she headed that way.

When she rounded the corner, he stopped still and his eyes went wide.

"What?" She glanced down at herself. Had she missed removing a tag?

"You look fantastic."

She relaxed and couldn't help but smile. The compliment warmed her straight through.

He moved closer. "I shouldn't be so shocked when you dress up like this."

He took her hands. "Seriously, Tasha. You're a knockout. It's a crying shame that you hide under baseball caps and boxy clothes."

His compliment warmed her, and she didn't know how to respond. She knew how she should respond—with annoyance at him for being shallow and disappointment in herself for succumbing to vanity. But that wasn't what she was feeling. She was feeling happy, excited, aroused. She'd dressed up for him, and he liked it.

"You're not so bad yourself," she said, her voice coming out husky.

He wore a tux better than anyone in the world.

"I don't want to share you," he said, drawing her closer.

"You think I'm yours to share?" She put a teasing lilt in her voice.

"You should be. You should be mine. Why aren't you mine, Tasha?" He searched her expression for a split second, and then his mouth came down on hers.

She knew there were all kinds of reasons that this was a bad idea. But she didn't have it in her. She wanted it as much as he did, maybe more. She wrapped her arms around his neck and returned his kiss.

She pressed her body against his. The arm at her waist held her tight. His free hand moved across her cheek, into her hair, cradling her face as he deepened the kiss. His leg nudged between hers, sending tendrils of desire along her inner thighs. Her nipples hardened against him, and a small pulse throbbed at her core.

He kissed her neck, nibbled her ear, his palm stroked up her spine, coming to the bare skin at the top of her back, slipping under the dress to caress her shoulder.

"Forget this," he muttered.

Then he scooped her into his arms and carried her farther into the house, down the hallway to his bedroom.

He dropped to the bed, bringing her with him, stretching her out in his arms, never stopping the path of his kisses.

"Matt?" she gasped, even as she inhaled his scent, gripped tight to his strong shoulders and marveled at how the world was spinning in a whole new direction. "The party."

Her body was on fire. Her skin craved his touch. Her lips couldn't get enough of his taste.

"Forget the party," he growled. "I need you, Tasha. I've imagined you in my bed so many, many times."

"I need you, too," she answered honestly.

It might have been the emotion of the past two days. Maybe it was the way he'd saved her. Maybe it was the intimacy of decorating for Christmas. Or maybe it was just hormones, chemistry. Matt wasn't like anyone she'd ever met.

He stripped off her dress and tossed his tux aside piece by piece.

When they were naked, they rolled together, wrapped in each other's arms.

She ended up on top. And she sat up, straddling him, smiling down.

"I have dreamed of this," he whispered, stroking his hands up her sides, moving to settle on her breasts.

"This might be a dream." She'd dreamed of him too,

too many times to count. If this was another, she didn't want to wake up.

"You might be a dream," he said. "But this isn't a dream. This is so real."

"It feels real to me." Unwilling to wait, she guided him inside, gasping as sensations threatened to overwhelm her. "Very, very, very real."

"Oh, Tasha," he groaned and pulled her close to kiss her.

She moved her hips, pleasure spiraling through her.

"Don't stop," he said, matching her motion.

"No way," she answered against his mouth.

She wanted to say more, but words failed her. Her brain had shut down. All she could do was kiss and caress him, drink in every touch and motion he made.

The world contracted to his room, to his bed, to Matt, beautiful, wonderful Matt.

She sat up to gaze at his gorgeous face. His eyes were opaque. His lips were dark red. His jaw was clenched tight. She captured his hand, lifted it to her face and drew one of his fingers into her mouth. Even his hands tasted amazing.

His other hand clasped her hips. He thrust harder, arching off the bed, creating sparks that turned to colors that turned to sounds. Lights flashed in her brain and a roar came up in her ears. Matt called her name over and over as she catapulted into an abyss.

Then she melted forward, and his strong arms went around her, holding her close, rocking her in his arms.

"That was..." he whispered in her ear.

"Unbelievable," she finished on a gasping voice.

"How did we do that? What's your magic?"

She smiled. "I thought it was yours."

"It's ours," he said.

Moments slipped by while they both caught their breaths.

"Are we still going to the party?" she asked.

"I'm not willing to share." He trailed his fingertips along her bare back.

She knew she should call him out for those words. But she was too happy, too content. She wasn't going to do anything to break the spell.

Ten

Matt resented real life. He wanted to lock himself away with Tasha and never come out. He'd held her in his arms all night long, waking to her smile, laughing with her over breakfast.

But she had insisted on going to work, and now he had a fire investigator sitting across from him in his office.

"Who was the last person to work on the engine before the fire?" Clayton Ludlow asked.

"My chief mechanic, Tasha Lowell. She's on her way here, but I can guarantee you she didn't make a mistake."

"I'm not suggesting she did. But I need to establish who had access to the engine room."

"After Tasha, I have no idea."

"You have security cameras?"

"I do."

"You reviewed the footage?" Clayton made some notes on a small pad of paper.

"Of course."

"Did anyone else board *Crystal Zone* the rest of the day?"

"Not that we could see. But Tasha thought..." Matt hesitated.

"Thought what?"

"She had a feeling someone was on board at the same time as her."

"Did she see someone?"

"No. It was just a feeling." And at this point, it was worrying Matt more than ever.

"There's nothing I can do with the *feeling* of another potential suspect."

"Tasha's not a suspect." Matt wanted the investigator to be clear on that.

Clayton's tone became brisk. "Are there blind spots left by the security cameras?"

"No."

Clayton's arched expression told Matt he was jumping to conclusions about Tasha.

"You know we've suspected sabotage," Matt said.

"I know. And we also know what started the fire."

Matt's interest ramped up. "How did he do it?"

"He *or she* left some oily rags in a pile. They ignited."

There was a knock on the door and Tasha pushed it open.

Matt waved her inside, and she took the vinyl guest chair next to Clayton.

Matt got straight to the point. "There were some oily rags left in the engine room. Any chance they were yours?"

He didn't believe for a minute they were, but he didn't want Clayton to think he was covering for Tasha. Not that he would need to. There was absolutely no way she was the saboteur.

"No," she said. "Never. Not a chance."

Matt looked to Clayton.

"How many boats do you work on in an average day?"

"One to six."

"So, you're busy."

"I'm busy," she said. "But I didn't forget something like that."

"How many boats did you work on the day of the fire?"

"Three." She paused. "No, four."

"This is a waste of time," Matt said.

Clayton ignored him. "The other problems Whiskey Bay has been having. I understand you were the last person to work on each of the engines."

"I was also the one to discover the wire short and the fuel leak that prevented the last fire." She slid a glance to Matt. It was obvious her patience was wearing.

Clayton made some more notes.

"Are you planning to charge me with something?" Tasha asked.

Her voice had gone higher, and her posture had grown stiff in the chair. Matt would have given anything to spirit her back to his house.

"Are you expecting to be charged with something?"

"No." She was emphatic.

Clayton didn't answer. He just nodded.

"We're wasting time," Matt said. "The real criminal is out there, and we're wasting time."

"Let me do my job," Clayton said.

"That's all we want." Matt nodded.

"It wasn't me," Tasha said.

"Noted. And now I have to finish my report." Clayton came to his feet.

Tasha stood, as well. "And I have engines to inspect. Think what you want about me," she said to Clayton. "But whoever is trying to hurt Matt's business is still trying to hurt Matt's business. If you don't want another disaster on your hands, help us find them."

She turned and left the office.

"Is she always so emotional?" Clayton asked.

"She's never emotional. And she's not emotional now. But I'm getting there." Matt rose. "Fill out your report. But if you pursue Tasha as a suspect or accomplice, you'll only be wasting valuable time."

Tasha paced her way down the pier, past the burned boats to *Monty's Pride*, which, thankfully, hadn't been damaged at all. She knew the inspector was only doing his job. But it was frustrating to have them spend so much time on her instead of looking for the real culprit. She had no doubt she'd be exonerated, no matter what people might believe right now. But she hated to think about the damage that could potentially be done in the meantime.

She heard the echoing sound of an open boat moving toward her. From the sound, she figured it was a small cartopper with a 150-horse outboard. Alex had chased a couple of reporters and a dozen lookie-loos away from the docks already this morning.

The red open boat was piloted by a man in a steel gray hoodie. He wasn't even wearing a life jacket.

"Jerk," she muttered under her breath, climbing down to the floater where it was obvious he was planning to dock.

"This is private property," she called out to him, waving him away.

He kept coming.

He didn't have a camera out yet; at least that was something.

She moved to the edge of the floater. "I said, this is private property."

He put a hand up to cup his ear.

He looked to be in his late fifties. He could be hard of hearing. Or it could simply be the noise of the outboard motor.

It was odd that he was wearing a hoodie. She associated them with teenagers, not older adults.

The boat touched broadside on the tire bumpers.

Tasha crouched to grasp the gunwale. "Is there something I can help you with?"

The man seemed oddly familiar.

"Have we met?" she asked, puzzled.

Maybe she'd been too quick to try to send him away. His business could be legitimate.

He shifted in his seat, coming closer to her.

And then she smelled it, the cologne or aftershave that she'd smelled the morning of the *Crystal Zone* fire.

"Only once," he said, raising an arm.

She jerked back, but she was too late.

Her world went dark.

It could have been minutes or hours later when she pushed her way to consciousness. She felt disoriented, and pain pulsed at her temples. Her first thought was to reach for Matt. She'd fallen asleep in his arms last night, and she wanted to wake up the same way.

She reached out, but instead of finding Matt, her hand hit a wall. No, it wasn't a wall. It was fabric. It was springy. It felt like the back of a sofa, and it had a musty smell.

She forced her eyes open, blinking in dim light.

The light was from a window up high in the room.

Her head throbbed harder, and she reached up to find a lump at her temple.

Then it all came back to her, the boat, the man, the smell. He'd hit her on the head. He'd knocked her out.

She sat up straight, pain ricocheting through her skull.

"You should have come home, Tasha." The voice was low and gravelly.

She looked rapidly around, trying to locate the source.

"Your mother misses you," he said.

She squinted at a shadowy figure in a kitchen chair across the room. "Who are you? Where am I? What do you want?"

"You're safe," he said.

She gave a hollow laugh. "I have a hard time believing that."

She gazed around the big room. It was more like a shed or a garage. She could make out a workbench of some kind. There were yard tools stacked against one wall, some sheers and a weed trimmer hanging on hooks.

"Where am I?" She put her feet on the floor, finding it was concrete.

The garage wasn't heated, and she was chilly.

"It's not important." He waved a dismissive hand. "We won't be here long."

"Where are we going?" Her mind was scrambling.

He'd pulled down his hoodie, but her vision was poor in the dim light. She'd thought she recognized him, but she couldn't place him. And she found herself wondering if she'd been mistaken.

But the cologne smell was familiar. It was… It was…

Her father's!

"Where's my dad?" she asked, sitting forward, debating her odds of overpowering the man.

He was older, but she was woozy, and her pounding headache was making her dizzy.

"He's in Boston. As always. Why would he be anywhere else?"

She wasn't going to give away that she'd made the cologne connection. It might give her some kind of advantage.

"No reason."

The man rose to his feet. "Tasha, Tasha, Tasha. You have proved so difficult."

She wished she knew how long she'd been here. Would Matt have noticed her missing yet? There'd be no tracks, nothing on the security cameras. The man had used a boat. That's how he'd got onto *Crystal Zone* without being seen yesterday morning. He'd come by water.

"You were the one who lit the oily rags," she said.

She couldn't tell for sure, but it looked as if he'd smiled.

"Used a candle as a wick," he said with a certain amount of pride in his voice, taking a few paces in front of her. "The wax just disappears." He fluttered his fingers. "For all anyone knows, they spontaneously combusted. Didn't anyone teach you the dangers of oily rags?"

"Of course they did. Nobody's going to believe I'd make a mistake like that."

"Well, it wouldn't have come to that—" now he sounded angry "—if you hadn't spent so much time cozying up to Matt Emerson. Otherwise you would have been fired days ago. I didn't see that one coming."

Tasha was speechless. Who was this man? How long had he been watching her? And what had he seen between her and Matt? As quickly as the thought formed, she realized that some stranger knowing she'd slept with Matt was the least of her worries.

She was in serious trouble here. She had no idea what this man intended to do with her.

Cold fear gripped the pit of her stomach.

"Have you seen Tasha?" Matt had found Alex on the pier next to *Orca's Run*, moving a wheeled toolbox.

"Not since this morning. Didn't she talk to the investigator?"

"That was three hours ago." Matt was starting to worry.

"Maybe she took a long lunch."

"Without saying anything?"

Alex gave him an odd look, and he realized his relationship with Tasha was far different from what everyone believed.

"Have you tried the Crab Shack?" Alex asked.

"That's a good idea."

Tasha had been getting to know Jules and Melissa recently. Matt liked that. He liked that she fit in with his circle of friends.

"Thanks," he said to Alex, waving as he strode down the pier. At the same time, he called Jules's cell phone, too impatient to wait until he got there.

"I don't know," Jules said when he asked the question. "I'm at home, feet up. They're really swollen today."

"Sorry to hear that."

"It's the price you pay." She sounded cheerful.

"Is Melissa at the restaurant?"

"I expect so. Is something wrong, Matt? You sound worried."

"I'm looking for Tasha."

Jules's tone changed. "Did something happen?"

"I don't know. She's not around. I can't find her on

the pier or in the main building. I checked the staff quarters and nothing."

"Maybe she went into town?"

"Not without telling me."

There was a silent pause. "Because of the fire?"

It was on the tip of his tongue to tell Jules he thought Tasha was the target. He might not have any proof, but his instincts were telling him somebody was out to discredit her. Heck, they already had the fire department thinking she was the culprit. But he didn't want to upset Jules. Her focus needed to be on her and the babies. She needed to stay relaxed.

"It's probably nothing." He forced a note of cheer into his voice. "I'll walk over to the Crab Shack myself. Or maybe she did go into town. She might have needed parts."

"I'll let you know if I hear from her," Jules said.

"Thanks. You relax. Take care of those babies."

Matt signed off.

He'd been walking fast, and he headed down the stairs to the parking lot.

"Matt!" It was Caleb, exiting his own car.

Matt trotted the rest of the way, hoping Caleb had news about Tasha.

Caleb was accompanied by an older woman.

"What is it?" he asked Caleb between deep breaths.

Caleb gestured to the fiftysomething woman. "This is Annette Lowell. She came to the Crab Shack looking for Tasha. She says she's her mother."

Matt didn't know how to react. Could Annette's appearance have something to do with Tasha being gone? "Hello."

The woman flashed a friendly smile. "You must be Matt Emerson."

"I am." Matt glanced at Caleb. He was beyond confused.

"Annette came to visit Tasha," Caleb said, his subtle shrug and the twist to his expression telling Matt he had no more information than that.

"Was Tasha expecting you?" Matt asked, still trying to pull the two events together. Was Tasha avoiding her mother? Matt knew they were estranged.

"No. I haven't spoken to Tasha in over a year."

"Not at all?"

"No."

Matt didn't really want to tell the woman her daughter was missing. He wasn't even sure if Tasha was missing. There could still be a logical explanation of why he couldn't find her.

"I saw the coverage of that terrible fire," Annette said to Matt. "I hope you'll be able to replace the yachts."

"We will."

"Good, good. I'm *so* looking forward to getting to know you." Her smile was expectant now. "I had no idea my daughter was dating such an accomplished man."

Dating? Where had Annette got the idea they were dating?

Then he remembered the picture in the national news, his arm around Tasha's shoulder, the expression of concern captured by the camera. Annette must have seen it and concluded that he and Tasha were together. It was clear she was happy about it.

"I'm a little busy right now." He looked to Caleb for assistance.

It wasn't fair to dump this on Caleb, but Matt had to concentrate on Tasha. He had to find her and assure himself she was safe. He was trying his house next. There was an outside chance she'd gone up there for a rest and turned off her phone. It was a long shot. But he didn't know what else to do.

Caleb stepped up. "Would you like to meet my wife?" he asked Annette. "She's pregnant and resting at the house right now, just up there on the hill. We're having twins."

Annette looked uncertain. It was clear she'd rather stay with Matt.

"Great idea," Matt chimed in. "I'll finish up here, and maybe we can talk later."

"With Tasha?" she asked.

"Of course."

The answer seemed to appease her, and she went willingly with Caleb.

Once again, Matt owed his friend big-time.

Without wasting another second, he called Melissa and discovered Tasha hadn't been to the Crab Shack in a couple of days. He checked his house but found nothing. So he asked the crew and dockworkers to check every inch of every boat.

They came up empty, and Matt called the police.

They told him he couldn't file a missing persons report for twenty-four hours. Then they had the gall to suggest Tasha might have disappeared of her own accord—because she knew she'd been caught committing arson.

It took every ounce of self-control he had not to ream the officer out over the phone.

His next stop was the security tapes from this morning. While he was reviewing them in the office, Caleb came back.

"What was *that* all about?" Caleb asked Matt without preamble.

"I have no idea. But I have bigger problems."

Caleb sobered. "What's going on?"

"It's Tasha. I can't find her."

"Was she supposed to be somewhere?"

"Here. She's supposed to be here!"

Caleb drew back.

"Sorry," Matt said. "I'm on edge. She's been missing for hours. The police won't listen."

"The *police*?"

"The fire department thinks she's an arsonist."

"Wait. Slow down."

"She was the last person known to be on board *Crystal Zone*. They concluded some oily rags combusted in the engine room, and they blame her for leaving them there—possibly on purpose."

"That's ridiculous," Caleb said.

"It's something else. It's someone else." Matt kept his attention on the security footage. "There she is."

Caleb came around the desk to watch with him.

Tasha walked down the pier. By the time clock, he knew it was right after she'd talked to the fire investigator. She'd disappeared behind *Monty's Pride*.

Matt waited. He watched and he waited.

"Where did she go?" Caleb asked.

"There's nothing back there." Matt clicked Fast-Forward, and they continued to watch.

"That's an hour," Caleb said. "Would she be working on *Monty's Pride*?"

"We checked. She's not there. And she couldn't have boarded from the far side."

"I hate to say it," Caleb ventured. "Is there any chance she fell in?"

Matt shot him a look of disbelief. "Really? Plus the tide's incoming." He had to steel himself to even say it out loud. "She wouldn't have washed out to sea."

"I'm stretching," Caleb said.

"Wait a minute." The answer came to Matt in a lightning bolt. "A boat. If she left the pier without coming back around, it had to have been in a boat."

"The Crab Shack camera has a different angle."

Matt grabbed his coat. "Let's go."

Tasha's head was still throbbing, but at least her dizziness had subsided. She was thirsty, but she didn't want to say or do anything that might upset the man who held her captive. When he turned, she could see a bulge in the waistband of his pants.

It could be a gun. It was probably a gun. But at least he wasn't pointing it at her.

If she could get back to full strength, and if he came close enough, she might be able to overpower him. She knew instinctively that she'd get only one chance. If she tried and failed, he might go for the gun or knock her out again or tie her hands.

He'd been pacing the far side of the garage for a long time.

"You need something else to wear," he said. His tone was matter-of-fact. He didn't seem angry.

"Why?" she dared ask.

"Because you look terrible, all tatty and ratty. Your mother wouldn't like that at all."

"You know my mother?"

His grin was somewhat sickly. "Do I know your mother? I know her better than she knows herself."

Struggling to keep her growing fear at bay, Tasha racked her brain trying to place the man. Had they met back in Boston? Why was he wearing her father's favorite cologne?

"Why did you want me to get fired?" she dared to ask.

"Isn't it obvious? Your mother misses you. You need to come home."

Come home. It sounded like home for him, too. *He must live in Boston.*

"You thought if Matt fired me, I'd move back to Boston?"

"Ah, Matt. The handsome Matt. You wore a nice dress that night."

Tasha turned cold again.

"You must have liked it. You looked like you liked it, all red and sparkly. You looked like your sister Madison."

"Where's Madison?" Tasha's voice came out on a rasp. Had this man done something to the rest of her family?

"What's with all the questions?" he chided. "If you want to see Madison, simply come home."

"Okay," she agreed, trying another tactic. "I'll come home. How soon can we leave?"

He stared at her with open suspicion. "I'm not falling for that."

"Falling for what? I miss Madison. And I miss Shelby. I'd like to see them. A visit would be nice."

"No, no, no." He shook his head. "That was too quick. I'm not stupid."

"I simply hadn't thought about it for a while," she tried.

"You're trying to trick me. Well, it won't work."

"I don't want to trick you." She gave up. "I honestly want to give you what you want. You've gone to a lot of trouble here. You must want it very badly."

"First, you need to change."

Her heart leaped in anticipation. Maybe he'd leave the garage. Maybe he'd go shopping for some clothes. If he left her alone, especially if he didn't tie her hands, she could escape. There had to be a way out of this place.

"It's in the car."

"What's in the car?"

"The red dress."

She was back to being frightened again. "How did you get the red dress?"

He looked at her like she was being dense. "It was in your room. I took it from your room. I'm disappointed you didn't notice. You should take more care with such an expensive gown. I had it cleaned."

Tasha's creep factor jumped right back up again. At the same time, she realized she hadn't even noticed the dress was gone. When she'd thought back on that night, making love with Matt had been foremost on her mind. The dress had faded to insignificance.

The security cameras covered the marina but the staff quarters were farther back, out of range. He'd obviously slipped in at some point.

"I'll get it," the man said, heading for the door.

"I'm not changing in front of you," she shouted out.

He stopped and pivoted. "I wouldn't expect you to, dear. Whatever you think of me, I am a gentleman."

"What's your name?" She braved the question, then held her breath while she waited for him to answer or get angry.

"Giles."

"And you're from Boston?"

"The West End, born and raised." He seemed to expect her to be impressed.

"That's very nice."

"I'll get your dress. We need to go now."

"Where are we going?"

He turned again, this time his eyes narrowed in annoyance, and she braced herself. "Pay attention, Tasha. We're going to Boston."

She shuddered at his icy expression. He couldn't get

her all the way to Boston as his prisoner. He'd have to drive. They couldn't board a plane.

It would be all but impossible to watch her every second. She'd escape. She'd definitely find a way to escape.

But what if he caught her? What would he do then?

Eleven

The Crab Shack security footage confirmed Matt's worst fears. The picture was grainy, but it showed Tasha being hauled into a boat and taken away.

"It's red," Caleb said, "but that's about as much detail as I'm getting."

"Probably a twenty-footer," Matt said. "There's no way they're leaving the inlet. That's something at least."

TJ arrived at the Crab Shack's office. "What's going on? Melissa said you were looking for Tasha."

"Somebody grabbed her," Matt said.

His instinct was to rush to his car and drive, but he didn't know where he was going. He should call the police, but he feared that would slow him down. He had to find her. He absolutely had to find her.

"What do you mean grabbed her?" TJ asked, his expression equal parts confusion and concern.

When Matt didn't answer, TJ looked to Caleb.

"Show him the clip," Caleb said.

Matt replayed it.

TJ swore under his breath.

"Matt thinks they won't leave the inlet," Caleb said.

"It's a red twenty-footer. He might have pulled it onto a trailer, but maybe not. Maybe it's still tied up somewhere on the inlet."

"There are a lot of red cartoppers out there," TJ said, but he was taking out his phone as he said it.

Matt came to his feet. "We should start with the public dock." He was glad to have a course of action.

"What about the police?" Caleb asked.

"Herb?" TJ said into the phone. "Can you get me a helicopter?"

Matt turned to TJ in surprise.

"Now," TJ said and paused. "That'll do." He ended the call and pointed to the screen. "Can someone copy that for me?"

"Melissa?" Caleb called out.

She immediately popped her head through the doorway.

"Can you help TJ print out what's on the screen?"

"I'm going to the public dock," Matt said. "You'll call me?" he asked TJ.

"With anything we find," TJ said.

Under normal circumstances, Matt would have protested TJ's actions. But these weren't normal circumstances. He didn't care what resources it took. He was finding Tasha.

"I'll talk to the police," Caleb said. "What about Tasha's mother?"

Both TJ and Melissa stared at Caleb in surprise. "She's up with Jules. She suddenly dropped by for a visit."

"Yes," Matt said. "Talk to her. It's really strange that she's here. She might know something."

Matt sprinted to his car and roared out of the parking lot, zooming up the hill to the highway and turning right for the public dock. He dropped his phone on the seat beside him, ready to grab it if anyone called.

The sun was setting, and it was going to be dark soon. He could only imagine how terrified Tasha must be feeling. She had to be okay. She *had* to be okay.

It took him thirty minutes to get to the public dock. He leaped over the turnstile, not caring who might come after him.

He scanned the extensive docking system, row upon row of boats. He counted ten, no, twelve small red boats.

"Sir?" The attendant came up behind him. "If you don't have a pass card, I'll have to charge you five dollars."

Matt handed the kid a twenty. "Keep the change."

"Sure. Okay. Thanks, man."

Matt jogged to the dock with the biggest concentration of red twenty-footers.

He marched out on the dock, stopping to stare down at the first one. He realized he didn't know what he was looking for. Blood on the seat? He raked a hand through his hair. *Please, no, not that.*

Even if he found the boat, what would that tell him? He wouldn't know which way they went. Did the kidnapper have a car? Maybe the attendant was his best bet. Maybe the kid had seen something.

His phone rang. It was TJ, and Matt put it to his ear. "Yeah?"

"We see a red boat. It's a possible match."

"Where?"

"Ten minutes south of you. Take Ring Loop Road, third right you come to."

"TJ." Matt wanted him to be right. He so wanted him to be right. "I'm looking at a dozen red twenty-footers here."

"He hit her on the head," TJ reminded him. "I don't think he'd risk carrying her unconscious through the public dock. And if she was awake, she might call out. This place is secluded. And the boat is only tied off at the bow. The stern line is trailing in the water, like somebody was in a hurry."

"Yeah. Okay." Matt bought into TJ's logic. "It's worth a shot."

"We'll keep going farther."

"Thanks." Matt headed back to his car.

He impatiently followed TJ's directions, finally arriving at the turnoff. He followed the narrow road toward the beach, shutting off his engine to silently coast down the final hill.

He could see a red boat at the dock. The tide was high, pushing it up against the rocky shore. There was an old building visible through the trees.

He crept around to the front of the building and saw a car with the trunk standing open. He moved closer, silent on his feet, listening carefully.

The building door swung open, and he ducked behind a tree.

Tasha appeared. Her mouth was taped. Her hands were behind her back. And she was wearing the red party dress. A man had her grasped tight by one arm.

She spotted the open trunk. Her eyes went wide with fear, as she tried to wrench herself away.

"Let her go!" Matt surged forward.

The man turned. He pulled a gun and pointed it at Matt.

Matt froze.

Tasha's eyes were wide with fear.

"You don't want to do this," Matt said, regretting his

impulsive actions. How could he have been so stupid as to barge up on the kidnapper with no plan?

"I know exactly what I want to do," the man returned in a cold voice.

"Let her go," Matt said.

"How about *you* get out of my way."

"You're not going to shoot her," Matt said, operating in desperation and on the fly. He could not let the guy leave with Tasha. "You went to too much trouble to get her here."

"Who said anything about shooting *her*?" The man sneered.

Matt heard sirens in the distance, and he nearly staggered with relief. "The police are on their way."

"Move!" the man yelled to Matt.

"No. You're not taking her anywhere."

The man fired off a round. It went wide.

"Every neighbor for ten miles heard that," Matt said. "You'll never get away. If you kill me, that's cold-blooded murder. If you let her go, maybe it was a misunderstanding. Maybe you drive away. Maybe, you let her go, and I step aside, and you drive off anywhere you want."

To Matt's surprise, the man seemed to consider the offer.

Matt took a step forward. "The one thing that's not happening here is you leaving with Tasha."

The sirens grew louder.

"Last chance," Matt said, taking another step.

The man's eyes grew wild, darting around in obvious indecision.

Then he shoved Tasha to the side.

She fell, and Matt rushed toward her and covered her with his body.

The kidnapper jumped into the car and zoomed off, spraying them with dust and stones.

As the debris settled, Matt pressed the number for TJ. Then he gently peeled the tape from Tasha's mouth. "Are you hurt?"

"He's getting away," she gasped.

"He won't." Matt put the phone to his ear.

TJ had a bird's-eye view, and he was obviously in touch with both Caleb and the police.

The call connected.

"Yeah?" TJ said.

"He's running, red car," Matt said to TJ. "I've got Tasha."

"We see him."

The helicopter whirled overhead.

"There's only one road out," Matt said to Tasha. "And TJ can see him from the air. There's no way for him to escape. Now, please tell me you're all right."

"I'm fine. Frightened. I think that man is crazy."

"Did he tell you what he wanted? Why are you dressed up? Never mind. Don't say anything. Just..." Matt removed his jacket and wrapped it around her shoulders. "Rest. Just rest."

He wrapped his arms around her, cradling her against his chest. All he wanted to do was hold her. Everything else could wait.

The small police station was a hive of activity. Matt hadn't left Tasha's side since he'd found her, and everything beyond him and the detective interviewing her was a blur of motion, muted colors and indistinct sounds.

"You said you might have recognized Giles Malahide?" the detective asked her for what she thought was about the tenth time.

"Why do you keep asking?" Matt interjected.

The detective gave him a sharp look. "I'm trying to get a full picture." He turned his attention to Tasha again. "You said he seemed familiar."

"His smell seemed familiar. He was wearing the same brand of cologne as my father. And he talked about my mother."

"What did he say about your mother?"

"That she missed me."

"Tasha, darling." It was her mother's voice.

Tasha gave her head a swift shake. She was in worse shape than she'd thought. She tightened her grip on Matt's hands, waiting for the auditory hallucination to subside.

"I *need* to see her." Her mother's voice came again. "I'm her *mother*."

Tasha's eyes focused on a figure across the room. It was her mother and she was attempting to get past two female officers.

"Matt?" Tasha managed in a shaky voice.

She looked to him. He didn't seem surprised. Her mother was here? Her mother was actually in the room?

"You called my mother?" she asked. "Why would you call my mother?"

"I didn't call her. She showed up asking for you."

"You said Giles Malahide talked about your mother?" the detective asked.

"Is that his full name?" Tasha asked. Not that it mattered. She really didn't care who he was, as long as he stayed in jail and got some help.

"What is *he* doing here?" Tasha's mother demanded.

Tasha looked up to see Giles Malahide being marched past in handcuffs.

Matt quickly put his arms around Tasha and pulled her against his shoulder.

"Annette," Giles called out. "Annette, I found her. I found her."

"Bring that woman here," the detective barked.

"Can we go somewhere private?" Matt asked the detective.

"Yes," he said. "This way."

They rose, and Matt steered Tasha away from the commotion, down a short hallway to an interview room, helping her sit in a molded plastic chair.

"What is going on?" Tasha managed.

"We're going to find out," the detective said. Then his tone became less brisk, more soothing. "I know you've gone through this already. But can you start from the beginning? From the first instance of what you believed to be sabotage?"

Tasha was tired.

"Is that necessary?" Matt asked. His tone hadn't moderated at all.

She put a hand on his forearm. "I can do it."

"Are you sure?"

"I'm sure."

She reiterated the entire story, from the water found in the fuel in *Orca's Run*, to her eerie feeling on board *Crystal Zone* before the fire, to her terror at the prospect of being thrown in the trunk of Giles's car.

As she came to the end, there was a soft knock on the door. It opened, and a patrolwoman leaned her head into the room. "Detective?" she asked.

"Come in, Elliott."

"We have a statement from Giles Malahide. It's delusional, but it corroborates everything Annette Lowell is saying."

"My *mother* knew about this?" Tasha couldn't accept that.

"No, no," Officer Elliott was quick to say. "Malahide acted on his own." She glanced to the detective, obviously unsure of how much to reveal.

"Go on," he said.

"Giles worked on the Lowell estate as a handyman."

"Estate?" the detective asked and looked to Tasha.

Officer Elliott continued, "They're the Vincent Lowell family, libraries, university buildings, the charity.

"Giles claims he's in love with Annette," Officer Elliott said. "And he believed her fondest wish was to have her daughter Tasha back in Boston in the family fold. He tracked Tasha down. He thought if she got fired from the Whiskey Bay Marina, she'd come home. When that didn't work, he took a more direct approach."

Tasha felt like she'd fallen through the looking glass. The officer's summary was entirely plausible, but it didn't explain how her mother had turned up in the middle of it all.

"Why is my mother here?" she asked.

"She saw your photo in the newspaper. The one taken at the fire. The story talked about Matt Emerson and his business and, well..." Officer Elliott looked almost apologetic. "She said she wanted to meet your boyfriend."

Tasha nearly laughed. She quickly covered her mouth and tipped her head forward to stifle the inappropriate emotion.

"Are you all right?" Matt's tone was worried.

"I'm fine. I'm..." She looked back up, shaking her head and heaving a sigh. "It's my mother." She looked at Matt. "She thinks you're a catch. She thinks I've found myself a worthy mate who will turn me into a responsible married woman." Tasha looked to Officer Elliott. "Her fondest wish isn't to have me back in Boston. Her fondest wish is to see me settled down, not rattling around engine parts and boat motors."

"Do we have a full confession?" the detective asked Officer Elliott.

"He's denied nothing. We have plenty to hold him on."

The detective closed his notebook. "Then we're done here. You're free to go, Ms. Lowell."

"Are you ready to see your mother?" Matt asked as they rose.

With all that had happened today, facing her mother seemed like the easiest thing she'd ever been asked to do. "As ready as I'll ever be."

"You're sure?"

"It's fine." Tasha had been standing up to her mother for years. She could do it again.

They made their way back to the crowded waiting room. Melissa, Noah, Jules, Caleb and Alex were all there. Tasha found herself glad to see them. It felt like she had a family after all, especially with Matt by her side.

Jules gave her a hug. "Anything you need," she said. "All you have to do is ask."

"I'm just glad it's over," Tasha said. "It would have been nice to have a less dramatic ending."

The people within hearing distance laughed.

"But at least we know what was going on," Jules said. "Everything can get back to normal now."

"Tasha." Her mother made her way through the small cluster of people. She pulled Tasha into a hug. "I was so worried about you."

"Hello, Mom."

Tasha swiftly ended the hug. They weren't a hugging family. She could only assume her mother had been inspired by Jules to offer that kind of affection.

"You look lovely," her mother said, taking in the dress.

"Thank you."

"Are you all right? I had no idea Giles would do something like that. Your father fired him months ago."

"It wasn't your fault," Tasha said.

Matt stepped in. "It's time to take Tasha home."

"Of course. Of course," Annette said. "We can talk later, darling."

If her mother had truly come looking for a reformed daughter with an urbane, wealthy boyfriend, she was going to be sadly disappointed.

While Tasha slept, Matt had installed Annette in another of his guest rooms. Then Caleb, the best friend a man could ever ask for, invited Annette to join him and Jules for dinner at the Crab Shack. Matt was now staring at the clutter of Christmas decorations, wondering if Tasha would feel up to finishing the job in the next few days, or if he should simply cart them all down to the basement for next year.

He heard a noise, and looked to find her standing at the end of the hall.

"You're up," he said, coming to his feet. Then he noticed she was carrying her gym bag. "What are you doing?"

"Back to the staff quarters," she said.

"Why?" He knew she had to go eventually. But it didn't have to be right away.

"Thanks for letting me stay here," she said, walking toward the front door.

"Wait. Whoa. You don't have to rush off. You're fine here. It's good."

The last thing he wanted was for her to leave. He'd hoped… Okay, so he wasn't exactly sure what he'd hoped. But he knew for certain this wasn't it.

"No, it's not good. The danger has passed, and things can go back to normal."

"Just like that?" He snapped his fingers.

"Just like nothing. Matt, what's got into you?"

He followed her to the entry hall. "Your mother's here, for one thing."

Tasha dropped the bag at her feet. "I know she's here. And I'll call her tomorrow. We can do lunch at her hotel or something. I'll explain everything. She'll be disappointed. But I'm used to that. She'll get over it. She has two other perfectly good daughters."

"I mean she's here, here," Matt said, pointing to the floor. "I invited her to stay in my other guest room."

Tasha's expression turned to utter astonishment. "Why would you do that?"

"Because she's your mother. And I thought you were staying here. It seemed to make sense." He knew they weren't on the best of terms, but Annette had come all the way across the country to see Tasha. Surely, they could be civil for a couple of days.

"That was a bad idea," Tasha said.

"She told me you hadn't seen her in years."

"It's not a secret."

"Don't you think this is a good chance?"

Tasha crossed her arms over her chest. "You know why she's here, right?"

"To see you."

"To see *you*. She thinks I found a good man. She thinks I've come to my senses, and I'm going to start planning my wedding to you any minute now."

"I think she misses you," Matt said honestly. He hadn't spent a lot of time with Annette, but her concern for Tasha seemed genuine.

"She came out here because of the picture in the paper."

"The picture that told her where to find you," he argued.

"The picture that she thought told her a wealthy man was in my life."

"Stay and talk to her." What Matt really meant was stay and talk with him. But he couldn't say that out loud. He hated the thought of her going back to that dim little room where she'd be alone, and then he'd be alone, too.

"I'll see her tomorrow," Tasha said.

He couldn't let her slip away like this. "What about us?"

She looked tired, and a little sad. "There isn't an us."

"There was last night."

"Last night was…last night. Our emotions were high."

He didn't buy it. "Our emotions are still high."

"The danger is over. I don't need to be here. And I don't need you taking my mother's side."

"I'm not taking her side."

She put her hand on the doorknob. "I appreciate your hospitality, and what you've done for my mom. But my life is my own. I can't let her change it, and I can't let you change it either."

"Staying in my guest room isn't changing your life."

"No? I already miss your bathtub."

He couldn't tell if she was joking. "That's another reason to stay."

"No, that's another reason to go. I'm tough, Matt. I'm sturdy and hardworking. I don't need bubbles and bath salts and endless gallons of hot water."

"There's no shame in liking bath salts."

"This Cinderella is leaving the castle and going back home."

"That's not how the story ends."

"It's how this story ends, Matt."

"Give us a chance."

"I have to be strong."

"Why does being strong mean walking away?"

"Not tonight, Matt. Please, not tonight."

And then she was gone. And he was alone. He wanted to go after her, but it was obvious she needed some time.

Through the night, Tasha's mind had whirled a million miles an hour. It had pinged from the kidnapping to her mother to Matt and back again. She'd been tempted to stay and spend the night with him, and the feeling scared her.

She'd been tempted by Matt, by everything about his lifestyle, the soaker tub the pillow-top bed. She'd even wanted to decorate his Christmas tree.

She was attracted to his strength, his support and intelligence, his concern and kindness. She'd wanted to throw every scrap of her hard-won independence out the window and jump headlong into the opulent life he'd built.

She couldn't let herself do that.

"Tasha?" Her mother interrupted her thoughts from across the table at the Crab Shack.

"Yes?" Tasha brought herself back to the present.

"I said you've changed."

"I'm older." Her mother looked older, too. Tasha hadn't expected that.

"You're calm, more serene. And that was a lovely dress you had on yesterday."

Tasha tried not to sigh. "It was borrowed."

"That's too bad. You should buy some nice things for yourself. Just because you have a dirty day job, doesn't mean you can't dress up and look pretty."

"I don't want to dress up and look pretty." Even as

she said the words, she acknowledged they were a lie. She'd wanted to dress up for Matt. She still wanted to look nice for him. As hard as she tried, she couldn't banish the feeling.

"I don't want to argue, honey."

"Neither do I." Tasha realized she didn't. "But I'm a mechanic, Mom. And it's not just a day job that I leave behind. I like being strong, independent, relaxed and casual."

"I can accept that."

The answer surprised Tasha. "You can?"

Her mother reached out and covered her hand. "I'm not trying to change you."

Tasha blinked.

"But how does Matt feel about that?"

"Everything's not about a man, Mom."

"I know. But there's nothing like a good man to focus a woman's priorities."

Tasha was nervous enough about Matt's impact on her priorities. "You mean mess with a woman's priorities."

"What a thing to say. When I met your father, I was planning to move to New York City. Well, he changed that plan right away."

"You exchanged a mansion in the Hamptons for a mansion in Beacon Hill?"

"What do you have against big houses?" Annette asked.

"It's not the house. It's the lifestyle. Would you have married a mechanic and moved to the suburbs?"

The question seemed to stump her mother.

"I'd do that in a heartbeat. It would suit me just fine. But I can't be someone's wife who spends all her time dressing up, attending parties, buying new yachts and decorating Christmas trees."

"It's not the same thing. I'd be moving down the ladder. You'd be moving up."

Tasha retrieved her hand. "I'm on a different ladder."

Her mother's eyes narrowed in puzzlement. "Not needing to work is a blessing. When you don't need to work, you can do whatever you want."

"I do need to work."

"Not if you and Matt—"

"Mom, there is no me and Matt. He's my boss, full stop."

Her mother gave a knowing smile. "I've seen the way he looks at you. And I can't help but hear wedding bells. And it has nothing to do with wishful thinking."

"Oh, Mom. Matt doesn't want to marry me."

Matt wanted to sleep with her, sure. And she wanted to sleep with him. But he was her boss not her boyfriend.

"Well, not yet," Annette said. "That's not the way it works, darling. If only you hadn't left home so soon. There's so much I could have taught you."

"Mom, I left home because I didn't want to play those games."

"They're the only games worth playing."

"Oh, Mom."

It was an argument they'd had dozens of times. But strangely, it didn't upset Tasha as much as it normally did. She realized, deep down, her mother meant well.

"I want you to keep in touch, honey. Okay?" Annette said.

"Okay." Tasha agreed with a nod, knowing it was time to move to a different relationship with her family. She wasn't caving to their wishes by any stretch, but her mother seemed a lot more willing to see her side of things. "I will."

Her mother's expression brightened. "Maybe even come for Christmas? You could bring Matt with you. He can meet your father and, well, you can see what happens from there."

Baby steps, Tasha told herself. "You're getting way ahead of yourself, Mom."

"Perhaps. But a mother can hope."

Twelve

Matt sat sprawled on a deck chair in front of his open fireplace. He normally loved the view from the marina building's rooftop deck. Tonight, the ocean looked bland. The sky was a weak pink as the sun disappeared, and dark clouds were moving in from the west. They'd hit the Coast Mountains soon and rain all over him.

He should care. He should go inside. He couldn't bring himself to do either.

Tasha had asked him to back off, and he'd backed off. And it was killing him to stay away from her.

Footsteps sounded on the outdoor staircase a few seconds before Caleb appeared.

"What's going on?" he asked Matt.

"Nothin'." Matt took another half-hearted drink of his beer.

Caleb helped himself to a bottle of beer from the compact fridge. "Where's Tasha?"

Matt shrugged. "I dunno."

Caleb twisted off his cap and took a chair. "I thought you two were a thing."

"We're not a thing." Matt wanted to be a thing. But

what Matt wanted and what he got seemed to be completely different.

"I thought she stayed with you last night."

"That was the night before. When she was in danger. Last night, she went home."

"Oh."

"Yeah. Oh."

Caleb fell silent, and the fire hissed against the backdrop of the lackluster tide.

"You practically saved her life," he said.

"I guess that wasn't enough."

"What the heck happened?"

TJ appeared at the top of the stairs. "What happened to who?"

"To Matt," Caleb said. "He's all lonesome and pitiful."

"Where's Tasha?" TJ asked. Like Caleb, he helped himself to a beer.

"I'm not doing that all over again," Matt said.

"What?" TJ asked, looking from Matt to Caleb and back again.

"Trouble in paradise," Caleb said.

"It wasn't paradise," Matt said. Okay, maybe it had been paradise. But only for a fleeting moment in time, and now he felt awful.

"You were her white knight," TJ said as he sat down. "I saw it from the air."

Matt raised his bottle to punctuate TJ's very valid point. "That jerk shot at me. There was actual gunfire involved."

"So what went wrong?" TJ asked.

"That's what I asked," Caleb said.

"I asked her to say. She wanted to leave."

"Her mom really likes you," Caleb said.

"That's half the problem."

"Did you tell her how you feel?" TJ asked.

"Yes," Matt answered.

"You told her you were in love with her?"

"Wait, what?" Caleb asked. "Did I miss something?"

"That's your wild theory," Matt told TJ.

He didn't even know why TJ was so convinced it was true.

Sure, okay, maybe someday. If he was honest, Matt could see it happening. He could picture Tasha in his life for the long term.

"You moved heaven and earth to rescue her," Caleb said.

"She was my responsibility. She's my employee. She was kidnapped while she was at work."

"I've never seen you panic like that," TJ said.

He pulled his chair a little closer to the fire. The world was disappearing into darkness around them, and a chill was coming up in the air.

"A crazed maniac hit Tasha over the head and dragged her off in a boat." How exactly was Matt supposed to have reacted? "You were the one who hired a chopper," he said to TJ.

"It seemed like the most expeditious way to cover a lot of ground."

"That doesn't make you in love with Tasha." Matt frowned. He didn't even like saying the words that connected Tasha with TJ.

"What would you do if I asked her out again?" TJ asked.

Matt didn't hesitate. "I'd respectfully ask you not to do that."

Caleb snorted.

"See what I mean?" TJ said to Caleb.

"That doesn't prove anything." Although Matt had to admit he was exaggerating only a little bit.

And it went for any other guy, as well. He didn't know what he might do if he saw her with someone else. She was *his*. She had to be his.

"I can see the light coming on." Caleb was watching Matt but speaking to TJ.

"Any minute now..." TJ said. "Picture her in a wedding dress."

An image immediately popped up in Matt's mind. She looked beautiful, truly gorgeous. She was smiling, surrounded by flowers and sunshine. And he knew in that instant he'd do anything to keep her.

"And how do you feel?" Caleb asked. The laughter was gone from his voice.

"Like the luckiest guy on the planet."

"Bingo," TJ said, raising his beer in a toast.

"You need to tell her," Caleb said.

"Oh, no." Matt wasn't ready to go that far.

"She needs to know how you feel," TJ said.

"So she can turn me down again? She doesn't want a romance. She wants her career and her independence. She wants everyone to think of her as one of the guys."

"She told you that?" Caleb asked.

"She did."

"Exactly that?" TJ asked.

"She said her life was her own, and I wasn't going to change it. She said this was how our story ended."

Caleb and TJ exchanged a look.

"Yeah," Matt said. "Not going to be a happily-ever-after." He downed the rest of his beer.

"Wuss," TJ said.

"Coward," Caleb said.

Matt was insulted. "A guy shot at me."

"Didn't even wing you," TJ said.

"That's nothing," Caleb said.

"It was something," Matt said.

TJ leaned forward, bracing his hands on his knees. "You still have to tell her how you feel."

"I don't *have* to do anything."

"Haven't we always had your back?" Caleb asked.

"I asked her to stay," Matt repeated. "She decided to go."

"You asked her to stay the night." TJ's tone made the words an accusation.

"I meant more than that."

"Then tell her more than that."

Caleb came to his feet. "Ask her to stay for the rest of your life."

"That's..." Matt could picture it. He could honestly picture it.

"Exactly what you want to do," TJ said.

Matt stared at his friends.

TJ was right. They were both right. He was in love with Tasha, and he had to tell her. Maybe she'd reject him, maybe she wouldn't. But he wasn't going down without one heck of a fight.

"You'll want to get a ring," TJ said.

"It always works better with a ring," Caleb said.

"It worked for Noah," Matt agreed. "Do you think I should ask her in front of everyone?"

"No!" TJ and Caleb barked out in unison.

"Noah was sure of the answer," TJ said.

"You guys think she's going to turn me down." That was depressing.

"We don't," Caleb said.

"Maybe," TJ said. "It would probably help to get a really great ring. You need a loan?"

"I don't need a loan."

Matt might not be able to purchase two new yachts on short notice. But he could afford an engagement ring. He could afford a dazzling engagement ring—the kind of ring no woman, not even Tasha, would turn down.

Tasha had found the solution to her problem. She hated it, but she knew it was right. What she needed to do was glaringly obvious. She wrote Matt's name on the envelope and propped her resignation letter against the empty brown teapot on the round kitchen table in her staff quarters unit.

Somebody would find it there tomorrow.

She shrugged into her warmest jacket, pulling up the zipper. Her big suitcase was packed and standing in the middle of the room. She'd stuffed as much as she could into her gym bag. Everything else was in the three cardboard boxes she'd found in the marina's small warehouse.

She should hand him the letter herself. She knew that. A better woman would say goodbye and explain her decision. But she was afraid of what would happen if she confronted him, afraid she might cry. Or worse, afraid she'd change her mind.

She'd dreamed of Matt for the past three nights, spectacular, sexy dreams where he held her tight and made her feel cherished and safe. She loved them while she slept, but it was excruciatingly painful to wake up. She'd spent the days working hard, focusing on the challenges in front of her, trying desperately to wear out both her body and her mind.

It hadn't worked. And it wasn't going to work.

She gazed around the empty room, steeling herself. Maybe she'd go to Oregon, perhaps as far as California.

It was warm there. Even in December, it was warm in California.

She looped her gym bag over her shoulder and extended the handle on her wheeled suitcase. But before she could move, there was a soft knock on her door.

Her stomach tightened with anxiety.

Her first thought was Matt. But it didn't sound like his knock. He wasn't tentative.

It came again.

"Hello?" she called out.

"It's Jules," came the reply.

Tasha hesitated. But she set down the gym bag and made her way to the door. She opened it partway, mustering up a smile. "Hi."

"How are you doing?"

"I'm fine."

"I thought you might come to the Crab Shack to talk."

"I've been busy." Tasha realized she was going to miss Jules, as well. And she'd miss Melissa. Not to mention Caleb and TJ. She barely knew Noah, but what she knew of him she liked. It would have been nice to get to know him better.

"Are you sure everything's okay?" Jules asked, the concern in her eyes reflected in her tone.

"Good. It's all good." Tasha gave a rapid nod.

"Yeah? Because I thought you might..." Jules cocked her head. "Do you mind if I come in?"

Tasha glanced back at her suitcase. It wasn't going to stay a secret for long. But she wasn't proud of the fact that she was sneaking off in the dark.

Jules waited, and Tasha couldn't think of a plausible excuse to refuse.

"Sure," she said, stepping back out of the way.

Jules entered. She glanced around the room and frowned. "What are you doing?"

"Leaving," Tasha said.

"Are you going home for Christmas?"

"No."

Jules was clearly astonished. "You're *leaving*, leaving?"

"Yes."

"You quit your job?"

Tasha's gaze flicked to the letter sitting on the table. "Yes."

Jules seemed to be at a loss for words. "I don't get it. What happened?"

"Nothing happened." Tasha picked up her gym bag again. "I really need to get going."

"Matt knows?" Jules asked.

Tasha wished she could lie. "He will."

Jules spotted the letter. "You wrote him a Dear John?"

"It's a letter of resignation." Tasha made a move for the door.

"You can't," Jules said, standing in her way.

"Jules, don't do this."

"You're making a mistake."

Jules took out her phone.

"What are you—"

Jules raised the phone to her ear. A second passed, maybe two, before she said, "She's leaving."

Tasha grabbed her suitcase, making to go around Jules.

But Jules backed into the door, leaning against it. "Tasha, that's who."

"Don't be ridiculous," Tasha said to Jules.

"Right *now*," Jules said. "Her suitcase is packed and everything."

"Seriously?" Tasha shook her head. This was getting out of hand.

Jules's eyes narrowed on Tasha. "I don't know how long I can do that."

"Jules, *please*." Tasha was growing desperate. She didn't trust herself with Matt. There was a reason she'd quit by letter.

"Hurry," Jules said into the phone. Then she ended the call and flattened herself against the door.

Tasha glanced around for an escape. She could jump out the window, but it was quite a drop on that side. And her big suitcase wouldn't fit through. She'd probably sprain an ankle, and Matt would find her in a heap on the pathway.

"What have you done?"

"You'll thank me," Jules said, but she didn't look completely confident.

"This is a disaster. We made *love*."

"You did?"

Tasha gave a jerky nod. "Do you know how embarrassing this is going to be?"

"I promise it won't be."

"It will." Tasha was growing frantic. "We have chemistry. We have *so* much chemistry. He practically saved my life. Do you know what that does to a woman's hormones? I'll never be able to resist him."

Now Jules looked baffled.

"Why resist him?"

"Because I'm not going to be *that* woman."

"What woman is that?"

"The woman who had a fling with her boss, who lost all credibility. I'd have to quit eventually. I might as well do it now while I still have my dignity. It's important to me."

"But at what cost to your future? Don't you want to be happy, Tasha?"

Someone banged on the door.

"Open up," Matt shouted from the other side.

Tasha took a step backward, nearly tripping on the suitcase. The gym bag slipped from her shoulder.

Jules moved to the side, and Matt pushed open the door.

He took in the suitcase and the empty room, and then zeroed in on Tasha.

"*What* are you doing?" His expression was part worry, part confusion.

"I'm resigning."

"Why?"

"You know why."

His eyes flashed with what looked like desperation. "I have no idea why."

"We can't go on like this, Matt."

"On like what? I did what you asked. I backed off."

"Yes, well…" She knew that was true, and she didn't dare admit that it hadn't helped. She still wanted him. She missed him. She…

Oh, no.

Not that.

She would *not* love Matt.

His expression turned to concern. "Tasha?" He closed the space between them. "You just turned white as a sheet."

"Go away," she rasped.

"I'm not going away." His hands closed gently around her arms.

Caleb appeared in the open doorway. "What's going on?"

"Shh," Jules hissed at him.

"Tasha." Matt's voice softened, and he stroked his palms along her arms. "Do you need to sit down?"

"No." She needed to leave, that's what she needed.

But she didn't want to leave. She wanted to fall into his arms. She wanted him to hold her tight. But she couldn't do it. It would only make things worse.

She loved him, and her heart was breaking in two.

He took her hands. "Tasha."

She gazed at their joined hands, feeling tears gather behind her eyes. Her throat went raw and her voice broke. "Please let me go."

"I can't do that."

TJ's voice sounded. "What did I—"

"Shh," Jules and Caleb said in unison.

Matt glanced over his shoulder. Then he looked into Tasha's eyes.

"They told me not to do it like this," he said. He lifted her hands, kissing her knuckles. "I'm not sure of your answer, and it would definitely work better with a ring."

Tasha squinted at him, trying to make sense of his words.

"But I love you, Tasha. I want you forever. I want you to marry me."

A roaring came up so fast in her ears, she was sure she couldn't have heard right.

She glanced past Matt to find Jules, Caleb and TJ all grinning.

"Wh-what?" she asked Matt.

"I love you," he repeated.

"I hate dresses." She found herself saying the first thing that came to her mind.

"Marry me in cargo pants," he said. "I don't care."

But she knew there was more to it than that. "You want

someone to go yacht shopping with you, to take to fancy balls, to decorate your stupid Christmas tree."

He laughed softly and drew her into his arms.

"I'll go yacht shopping with him," Caleb offered.

"I'll go, too," TJ said. "After all, I'm the guy fronting the money."

"Let her speak," Jules said to both of them.

"You haven't thought this through," Tasha said.

"This is why you don't do it in front of people," Caleb whispered.

Jules elbowed him in the ribs.

"I've thought it through completely," Matt said.

She could see he was serious, and hope rose in her heart. She wanted to dream. She wanted to believe. Her voice went softer. "What if you change your mind?"

He arched a skeptical brow. "Change my mind about loving you?"

"About marrying a woman in cargo pants."

He drew back and cradled her face between his palms. "Tasha, I love you *exactly* the way you are."

Her heart thudded hard and deep inside her chest. She loved him, and she felt sunshine light up her world.

"I can't imagine my life without you and your cargo pants," he said.

Her heart lifted and lightened, and her lips curved into a gratified smile. "I suppose I could wear one more dress." She paused. "For the wedding."

His grin widened. "Is that a yes?"

She nodded, and he instantly wrapped her in a tight hug.

A cheer went up behind him.

"Yes," she whispered in his ear.

He kissed her then, deeply and passionately.

"Congratulations," TJ called out.

Matt laughed in clear delight as he broke the kiss. He kept one arm around Tasha, turning to his friends. "You could have given me some privacy."

"Are you kidding?" Caleb asked. "We were dying to see how this turned out."

"It turned out great," Matt said, giving Tasha a squeeze.

Jules moved forward. "Congratulations." She commandeered Tasha for a hug.

"You were right," Tasha said to her.

"Right about what?"

"I do thank you."

Jules smiled. "I knew it! I'm so happy for you, for both of you."

"I can't believe this has happened," Tasha managed, still feeling awestruck.

"I can't believe she didn't say it," Caleb put in.

"She did," Matt said. He pointed to his friends. "You all saw her nod. That's good enough for me. I have witnesses."

"The I-love-you part," Caleb said.

Matt looked to Tasha, showing surprise on his face. "You did. Didn't you?"

"I don't remember." She made a show of stalling.

"You don't remember if you love me?"

She teased. "I don't remember if I said it." She felt it with all her heart, and she couldn't wait to say it out loud. "I do love you, Matt. I love you so very much."

He scooped her up into his arms. "Good thing you're already packed." He started for the door.

"I've got the bags," TJ said.

Tasha couldn't help but laugh. She wrapped her arms around Matt's neck and rested her head against his shoulder. She was done fighting. They were going home.

* * *

It was late Christmas Eve, and Tasha stepped back to admire her handiwork on the tree.

Returning from the kitchen, two mugs of peppermint hot chocolate in his hands, Matt paused. He'd never seen a more amazing sight—his beloved fiancée making his house feel like the perfect home.

"We finally got it decorated," she said, turning her head to smile at him. "Yum. Whipped cream."

"Only the best," he said.

She was dressed in low-waisted black sweatpants, a bulky purple sweater and a pair of gray knit socks. Her hair was up in a ponytail, and she couldn't have looked more beautiful.

He moved forward, handing her one of the mugs. "It tastes fantastic."

"Thanks." She took a sip through the froth of whipped cream.

"And so do you." He kissed her sweet mouth.

"And not a ball gown in sight."

"This is better than any old ball."

"Music to my ears." She moved around the coffee table to sit on the sofa.

It was the moment he'd been waiting for. "Look at the time."

She glanced to the wall clock. "It's midnight."

"Christmas Day," he said.

She smiled serenely up at him. "Merry Christmas."

He set his mug down on the table and reached under the tree. "That means you can open a present."

Her smile faded. "We're not going to wait until morning?"

"Just one," he said, retrieving it.

He moved to sit beside her, handing over a small mint-green satin pouch. It was embossed in gold and tied with a matching gold ribbon.

"This is beautiful." She admired the package for a moment. Then she grinned like a little kid, untying the ribbon and pulling open the pouch.

His chest tightened with joy and anticipation.

She peeked inside. "What?" Then she held out her palm and turned the little bag over.

A ring dropped out—a two-carat diamond surrounded by tiny deep green emeralds that matched her irises.

"Oh, Matt." Her eyes shimmered as she stared at it. "It's incredible."

He lifted it from her palm. "You're what's incredible."

He took her left hand. "Tasha Lowell. I love you so much." He slipped the ring onto her finger. "I cannot wait to marry you."

"Neither can I." She held out her hand, admiring the sparkle. "This is perfect."

"You're perfect."

"Stop doing that."

"What?"

"One-upping my ring compliments."

"The ring can't hold a candle to you." He drew her into his arms and gave her a long, satisfying kiss.

By the time they drew apart, they were both breathless.

"So, what now?" she asked, gazing again at the glittery ring.

"Now we plan a wedding. You want big and showy? Or small with just our friends? We can elope if you want." Matt didn't care how it got done, just so long as it got done.

"My mom would die for a big wedding."

He smoothed her hair from her forehead. "You called

her back, didn't you?" He hadn't wanted to ask, not knowing how Tasha was feeling about her mother's renewed interest in her life.

"This afternoon."

"Did it go okay?"

Tasha shrugged. "She hasn't changed. But I get it, and I can cope. She's completely thrilled about you, remember? I imagine she'll be taking out an ad in the *Boston Globe* in time for New Year's."

"Do you mind?"

He'd support whatever Tasha wanted to do about her relationship with her mother.

"It feels good to make peace." She paused. "I suppose it wouldn't hurt to make them happy."

He searched her expression. "Are you actually talking about a formal wedding?"

A mischievous smile came across her face. "We could let Mom go to town."

Matt put a hand on Tasha's forehead, pretending to check for a fever.

"I could dress up," she said. "I could do the glitz-and-glamour thing for one night. As long as I end up married to you when it's over."

"You would look stupendous." He couldn't help but picture her in a fitted white gown, lots of lace, shimmering silk or satin.

"You'd like it, wouldn't you?"

"I would not complain."

"Then let's do it."

He wrapped her in another tight hug. "When I picture our future, it just gets better and better."

"Next thing you know, we'll be having babies."

"With you," he said. "I definitely want babies." He

pictured a little girl in front of the Christmas tree looking just like Tasha.

Maybe it was Jules's being pregnant, but he suddenly found himself impatient. He put a gentle hand on Tasha's stomach, loving the soft warmth. "How soon do you think we might have them?"

"I don't know." She reached out and popped the top button on his shirt. Then she opened another and another. "Let's go find out."

* * * * *

Can a former bad boy and the woman
he never forgot find true love during
one unforgettable Christmas?
Find out in CHRISTMASTIME COWBOY,
the sizzling new COPPER RIDGE *novel from*
New York Times *bestselling author Maisey Yates.*
Read on for your sneak peek...

Liam Donnelly was nobody's favorite.

Though being a favorite in their household growing up would never have meant much, Liam was confident that as much as both of his parents disdained their younger son, Alex, they hated Liam more.

And as much as his brothers loved him—or whatever you wanted to call their brand of affection—Liam knew he wasn't the one they'd carry out if there was a house fire. That was fine too.

It wasn't self-pity. It was just a fact.

But while he wasn't anyone's particular favorite, he knew he was at least one person's least favorite.

Sabrina Leighton hated him with every ounce of her beautiful, petite being. Not that he blamed her. But considering they were having a business meeting today, he did hope that she could keep some of the hatred bottled up.

Liam got out of his truck and put his cowboy hat on, surveying his surroundings. The winery spread was beautiful, with a large, picturesque house overlooking the grounds. The winery and the road leading up to it were carved into an Oregon mountainside. Trees and forest surrounded the facility on three sides, creating a secluded feeling. Like the winery was part of another world. In front of the first renovated barn was a sprawling lawn and a path that led down to the river. There was a seating area there and Liam knew that during the warmer months it was a nice place to hang out. Right now, it was too damned cold, and the damp air that blew up from the rushing water sent a chill straight through him.

He shoved his hands into his pockets and kept walking. There were three rustic barns on the property that they used for weddings and dinners, and one that had been fully remodeled into a dining and tasting room.

He had seen the new additions online. He hadn't actually been to Grassroots Winery in the past thirteen years. That was part of the deal. The deal that had been struck back when Jamison Leighton was still owner of the place.

Back when Liam had been nothing more than a good-for-nothing, low-class troublemaker with a couple of misdemeanors to his credit.

Times changed.

Liam might still be all those things at heart, but he was also a successful businessman. And Jamison Leighton no longer owned Grassroots.

Some things, however, hadn't changed. The presence of Sabrina Leighton being one of them.

It had been thirteen years. But he couldn't pretend he thought everything was all right and forgiven. Not considering the way she had reacted when she had seen him at Ace's bar the past few months.

Small towns. Like everybody was at the same party and could only avoid each other for so long.

If it wasn't at the bar, they would most certainly end

up at a four-way stop at the same time, or in the same aisle at the grocery store.

But today's meeting would not be accidental. Today's meeting was planned. He wondered if something would get thrown at him. It certainly wouldn't be the first time.

He walked across the gravel lot and into the dining room. It was empty, since the facility—a rustic barn with a wooden chandelier hanging in the center—had yet to open for the day. There was a bar with stools positioned at the front, and tables set up around the room. Back when he had worked here, there had been one basic tasting room, and nowhere for anyone to sit. Most of the wine had been sent out to retail stores for sale, rather than making the winery itself some kind of destination.

He wondered when all of that had changed. He imagined it had something to do with Lindy, the new owner and ex-wife of Jamison Leighton's son, Damien. As far as Liam knew, and he knew enough—considering he didn't get involved with business ventures without figuring out what he was getting into—Damien had drafted the world's dumbest prenuptial agreement. At least, it was dumb for a man who clearly had problems keeping his dick in his pants.

Though why Sabrina was still working at the winery when her sister-in-law had current ownership, and her brother had been deposed, and her parents were—from what he had read in public records—apoplectic about the loss of their family legacy, he didn't know. But he assumed he would find out. At about the same time he found out whether or not something was going to get thrown at his head.

The door from the back opened, and he gritted his teeth. Because, no matter how prepared he felt philosophically to see Sabrina, he knew that there would be impact. There always was. A damned funny thing, that one woman could live in the back of his mind the way she had for so long. That no matter how many years or how many women he put between them, she still burned bright and hot in his memory.

That no matter that he had steeled himself to run into her—because he knew how small towns worked—the impact was like a brick to the side of his head every single time.

She appeared a moment after the door opened, looking severe. Overly so. Her blond hair was pulled back into a high ponytail, and she was wearing a black sheath dress that went down past her knees but conformed to curves that were more generous than they'd been thirteen years ago.

In a good way.

"Hello, Liam," she said, her tone impersonal. Had she not used his first name, it might have been easy to pretend that she didn't know who he was.

"Sabrina."

"Lindy told me that you wanted to talk about a potential joint venture. And since that falls under my jurisdiction as manager of the tasting room, she thought we might want to work together."

Now she was smiling.

The smile was so brittle it looked like it might crack her face.

"Yes, I'm familiar with the details. Particularly since this venture was my idea." He let a small silence hang there for a beat before continuing. "I'm looking at an empty building on the end of Main Street. It would be more than just a tasting room. It would be a small café with some retail space."

"How would it differ from Lane Donnelly's store? She already offers specialty foods."

"Well, we would focus on Grassroots wine and Laughing Irish cheese. Also, I would happily purchase products from Lane's to give the menu a local focus. The café would be nothing big. Just a small lunch place with wine. Very limited selection. Very specialty. But I feel like in a tourist location, that's what you want."

"Great," she said, her smile remaining completely immobile.

He took that moment to examine her more closely. The changes in her face over the years. She was more beautiful now than she had been at seventeen. Her slightly round, soft face had refined in the ensuing years, her cheekbones now more prominent, the angle of her chin sharper.

Her eyebrows looked different too. When she'd been a teenager, they'd been thinner, rounder. Now they were a bit stronger, more angular.

"Great," he returned. "I guess we can go down and have a look at the space sometime this week. Gage West is the owner of the property, and he hasn't listed it yet. Handily, my sister-in-law is good friends with his wife. Both of my sisters-in-law, actually. So I got the inside track on that."

Her expression turned bland. "How impressive."

She sounded absolutely unimpressed. "It wasn't intended to be impressive. Just useful."

She sighed slowly. "Did you have a day of the week in mind to go view the property? Because I really am very busy."

"Are you?"

"Yes," she responded, that smile spreading over her

face again. "This is a very demanding job, plus I do have a life."

She stopped short of saying exactly what that life entailed.

"Too busy to do this, which is part of your actual job?" he asked.

On the surface she looked calm, but he could sense a dark energy beneath that spoke of a need to savage him. "I had my schedule sorted out for the next couple of weeks. This is coming together more quickly than expected."

"I'll work something out with Gage and give Lindy a call, how about that?"

"You don't have to call Lindy. I'll give you my phone number. You can call or text me directly."

She reached over to the counter and took a card from the rustic surface, extending her hand toward him. He reached out and took the card, their fingertips brushing as they made the handoff.

And he felt it. Straight down to his groin, where he had always felt things for her, even though it was impossible. Even though he was all wrong for her. And even though now they were doing a business deal together, and she looked like she would cheerfully chew through his flesh if given half the chance.

She might be smiling, but he didn't trust that smile. He was still waiting. Waiting for her to shout recriminations at him now that they were alone. Every other time he had encountered her over the past four months it had been in public. Twice in Ace's bar, and once walking down the street, where she had made a very quick sharp left to avoid walking past him.

It had not been subtle, and it had certainly not spoken of somebody who was over the past.

So his assumption had been that if the two of them were ever alone she was going to let him have it. But she didn't. Instead, she gave him that card and then began to look…bored.

"Did you need anything else?" she asked.

"Not really. Though I have some spreadsheet information that you might want to look over. Ideas that I have for the layout, the menu. It is getting a little ahead of ourselves, in case we end up not liking the venue."

"You've been to look at the venue already, haven't you?" It was vaguely accusatory.

"I have been there, yes. But again, I believe in preparedness. I was hardly going to get very deep into this if I didn't think it was viable. Personally, I'm interested in making sure that we have diverse interests. The economy doesn't typically favor farms, Sabrina. And that is essentially what my brothers and I have. I expect an uphill fight to make that place successful."

She tilted her head to the side. "Like you said, you do your research."

Her friendliness was beginning to slip. And he waited. For something else. For something to get thrown at him. It didn't happen.

"That I do. Take these," he said, handing her the folder that he was holding on to. He made sure their fingers didn't touch this time. "And we'll talk next week."

Then he turned and walked away from her, and he resisted the strong impulse to turn back and get one more glance at her. It wasn't the first time he had resisted that.

He had a feeling it wouldn't be the last.

As soon as Liam walked out of the tasting room, Sabrina let out a breath that had been killing her to keep in. A breath that contained about a thousand insults and recriminations. And more than a few very colorful swear word combinations. A breath that nearly burned her throat, because it was full of so many sharp and terrible things.

She lifted her hands to her face and realized they were shaking. It had been thirteen years. Why did he still affect her like this? Maybe, just maybe, if she had ever found a man who made her feel even half of what Liam did, she wouldn't have such a hard time dealing with him. The feelings wouldn't be so strong.

But she hadn't. So that supposition was basically moot.

The worst part was the tattoos. He'd had about three when he'd been nineteen. Now they covered both of his arms, and she had the strongest urge to make them as familiar to her as the original tattoos had been. To memorize each and every detail about them.

The tree was the one that really caught her attention. The Celtic knots, she knew, were likely a nod to his Irish heritage, but the tree—whose branches she could see stretching down from his shoulder—she was curious about what that meant.

"And you are spending too much time thinking about him," she admonished herself.

She shouldn't be thinking about him at all. She should just focus on congratulating herself for saying nothing stupid. At least she hadn't cried and demanded answers for the night he had completely laid waste to her every feeling.

"How did it go?"

Sabrina turned and saw her sister-in-law, Lindy, come in. People would be forgiven for thinking that she and Lindy were actually biological sisters. In fact, they looked much more alike than Sabrina and her younger sister, Beatrix, did.

Like Sabrina, Lindy had long, straight blond hair. Bea, on the other hand, had freckles all over her face and a wild riot of reddish-brown curls that resisted taming almost as strongly as the youngest Leighton sibling herself did.

That was another thing Sabrina and Lindy had in common. They were predominantly tame. At least, they kept things as together as they possibly could on the surface.

"Fine."

"You didn't savage him with a cheese knife?"

"Lindy," Sabrina said, "please. This is dry-clean only." She waved her hand up and down, indicating her dress.

"I don't know what your whole issue is with him..."

Because no one spoke of it. Lindy had married Sabrina's brother after the unpleasantness. It was no secret that Sabrina and her father were estranged—even if it was a brittle, quiet estrangement. But unless Damien had told Lindy the details—and Sabrina doubted he knew all of them—her sister-in-law wouldn't know the whole story.

"I don't have an issue with him," Sabrina said. "I knew him thirteen years ago. That has nothing to do with now. It has nothing to do with this new venture for the winery. Which I am on board with one hundred percent." It was true. She was.

"Well," Lindy said, "that's good to hear."

She could tell that Lindy didn't believe her. "It's going to be fine. I'm looking forward to this." That was also true. Mostly. She was looking forward to expanding Grassroots. Looking forward to helping build the winery, and making it into something that was truly theirs. So that her parents could no longer shout recriminations about Lindy stealing something from the Leighton family.

Eventually, they would make the winery so much more successful that most of it would be theirs.

And if her own issues with her parents were tangled up in all of this, then…that was just how it was.

Sabrina wanted it all to work, and work well. If for no other reason than to prove to Liam Donnelly that she was no longer the seventeen-year-old girl whose world he'd wrecked all those years ago.

In some ways, Sabrina envied the tangible ways in which Lindy had been able to exact revenge on Damien. Of course, Sabrina's relationship with Liam wasn't anything like a ten-year marriage ended by infidelity. She gritted her teeth. She did her best not to think about Liam. About the past. Because it hurt. Every damn time it hurt. It didn't matter if it should or not.

But now that he was back in Copper Ridge, now that she sometimes just happened to run into him, it was worse. It was harder not to think about him.

Him and the grand disaster that had happened after.

***

Look for CHRISTMASTIME COWBOY,
available from Maisey Yates and HQN Books
wherever books are sold.

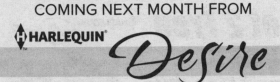

SPECIAL EXCERPT FROM

Bane Westmoreland's SEAL team is made up of sexy alpha males.

Don't miss Laramie "Coop" Cooper's story
HIS SECRET SON
from New York Times *bestselling author Brenda Jackson!*

The SEAL who fathered Bristol's son died a hero's death…or so she was told. But now Coop is back and vowing to claim his child! Her son deserves to know his father, so Bristol must find a way to fight temptation…and keep her heart safe.

Read on for a sneak peek at
HIS SECRET SON,
part of ***THE WESTMORELAND LEGACY*** *series.*

Laramie stared at Bristol. "You were pregnant?"

"Yes," she said in a soft voice. "And you're free to order a paternity test if you need to verify that my son is yours."

He had a son? It took less than a second for his emotions to go from shock to disbelief. "How?"

She lifted a brow. "Probably from making love almost nonstop for three solid days."

They had definitely done that. Although he'd used a condom each and every time, he knew there was always a possibility that something could go wrong.

"And where is he?" he asked.

"At home."

HDEXP1117

Where the hell was that? It bothered him how little he knew about the woman who'd just announced she'd given birth to his child. At least she'd tried contacting him to let him know. Some women would not have done so.

If his child had been born nine months after their holiday fling, that meant he would have turned two in September. While Laramie was in a cell, somewhere in the world, Bristol had been giving life.

To his child.

Emotions Laramie had never felt before suddenly bombarded him with the impact of a Tomahawk missile. He was a parent, which meant he had to think about someone other than himself. He wasn't sure how he felt about that. But then, wasn't he used to taking care of others as a member of his SEAL team?

She nodded. "I'm not asking you for anything Laramie, if that's what you're thinking. I just felt you had a right to know about the baby."

She wasn't asking him for anything? Did she not know her bold declaration that he'd fathered her child demanded everything?

"I want to see him."

"You will. I would never keep Laramie from you."

"You named him Laramie?" Even more emotions swamped him. Her son—their son—had his name?

She hesitated. "Yes."

Then he asked, "So, what's your reason for giving yourself my last name, as well?"

HDEXP1117

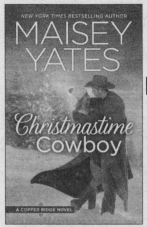